HORSES OF

HALF MOON
RANCH

SILVER SPUR

Also by Jenny Oldfield
published by Hodder Children's Books

HORSES OF
HALF MOON
RANCH

SILVER SPUR

JENNY OLDFIELD

Illustrated by
Paul Hunt

Hodder
Children's
Books

a division of Hodder Headline Limited

With thanks to Bob, Karen and Katie Foster, and to the staff and guests at Lost Valley Ranch, Deckers, Colorado

Copyright © 2001 Jenny Oldfield
Illustrations copyright © 2001 Paul Hunt

First published in Great Britain in 2001
by Hodder Children's Books

The right of Jenny Oldfield to be identified as the author of
this work has been asserted by her in accordance with the
Copyright, Designs and Patents Act 1988.

10 9 8 7 6 5 4 3 2 1

A Catalogue record for this book is available from the British Library

ISBN 0 340 79169 1

Typeset by Avon Dataset Ltd, Bidford-on-Avon, Warks

Printed and bound in Great Britain by
The Guernsey Press Co. Ltd, Channel Isles

Hodder Children's Books
a division of Hodder Headline Limited
338 Euston Road
London NW1 3BH

1

Kirstie Scott hated goodbyes. They left her at a loose end and made her sad, especially when it was goodbye to someone who had been a part of the scene at Half-Moon Ranch. Almost family in fact.

'Bye, Charlie.' Kirstie's mom, Sandy, put her arms around the young wrangler and held him tight. 'You take care, OK!'

Charlie nodded. 'Thanks for everything. I've had such a good time working with you guys at the ranch.'

Grabbing his bag and slinging it over his shoulder, he studied the electronic Departures board at the entrance to Terminal C in Denver International Airport.

'The flight to Ohio leaves from Gate 24,' Matt told him quietly.

He and Charlie went way back. They'd been at school together in Denver, then Charlie had gone away to college. After a couple of years he'd come back to Colorado and chilled out at the Scotts' place. He'd planned to stay a few weeks, maybe doing odd-jobs to earn his keep. But the weeks had turned into months and then a year. And the college drop-out had become an excellent wrangler, working with the Scotts' herd of quarter-horses and leading the guests on trail-rides.

But now Charlie reckoned it was time to go back to Ohio State and graduate. Reluctantly he'd decided to hang up his stetson and store his cowboy boots in the loft above the barn.

'We've loved having you stay with us,' Sandy assured him. 'You be sure to come back and visit any time.'

Hanging back in the rear of the group, Kirstie felt herself begin to choke up. There would be no more 'Hey, Charlie!' as she crossed the yard at dawn, no more partnering him at the square dance in the evening after a long day out on the trail, and no more hauling hay bales, scooping poop or driving the tractor out into Red Fox Meadow with her shy, kind friend.

As Charlie worked out his route through the busy airport, Matt reminded him that he only had ten minutes to get to the check-in gate.

'So I guess this is it,' he told them. He put up his hand to Kirstie in a final high-five gesture. 'Hey,' he told her. 'You take care of you, too.'

As she met his hand, her effort to smile crumpled. 'We're gonna miss you,' she murmured.

'Me too.'

And that was it. Charlie was turning away, striding out across the marble floor, under the futuristic peaked canopy of the airport's central plaza, heading for a new life which had no place in it for horses or ranches or the wide open spaces of the Meltwater Range.

Sandy was the one who took a deep breath and picked their spirits up off the polished floor.

'Let's go and say hi to the guys in Terminal A,' she said briskly.

As one door closed, another opened.

Goodbye, Charlie Miller; hello Troy Hendren: wading through the crowd in Arrivals dressed in a red shirt, blue jeans and cowboy boots, his white stetson easily visible over the bald heads and baseball caps of much shorter passengers. Behind him, almost but not quite as tall, came Sandy's boyfriend, Brad Martin.

'Jeez, am I glad to get off of that plane!' Picking out his new employer, Troy did away with the introductions. He strode quickly towards Sandy, Matt and Kirstie, holding out a broad, hard-worked hand that was scarred and roughened with callouses across the palm. 'Never did like airplanes as a way of getting from A to B,' he said in a loud voice, his accent carrying a broad western twang. 'Man, I take a look at those jet engines and say to myself, "No way, no sir!" It ain't natural!'

A smiling Sandy shook Troy's hand.

Kirstie noticed that beside the rangy new wrangler, her mom looked small, slight and not at all like the boss of a ranch. Too feminine with her long, fair hair. Not tough enough to hold her own against an ornery cowboy from the Montana plains. A walkover, in fact.

She soon picked up that this was the way Troy saw things too. 'So, I hear you need an expert cowhand to bring in those spring steers,' he began condescendingly, leading the way across the concourse towards the carpark. 'Ain't a job for an amateur, I gotta admit.'

Seeing Sandy bridle, Kirstie grinned at Matt.

'No, ma'am. What you need and what you got here is a real live cowboy!' Troy went on. 'I bin workin' steers all my life, since I was knee-high to a grasshopper. Ain't nothin' I don't know about cuttin' and ropin', even if I say so myself.'

'Yeah, Brad gave you a pretty good endorsement when I asked him about you,' Sandy told him, quietly biding her time. Gathering speed, she stepped ahead of the new arrival to steer him gently towards the bay where the ranch station wagon was parked.

'I'm happier on horseback than in anything with wheels or wings,' Troy went on, climbing into the back seat of the car and folding up his long legs to squeeze in. 'Ain't a horse in this world I don't understand; it's like we speak the same language. Good communication, that's the secret of horsemanship. You give your mount the right kind of signals, he'll do just about anythin' you tell him.'

'Sounds like you and my daughter will have a lot in common,' Sandy said, making the belated introduction.

Kirstie nodded as she joined Troy in the back

seat. The new guy gave off the solid aura of a true, old-fashioned cowboy, but his brash style didn't fit Kirstie's image of the strong, silent type. In fact, if she was honest, so far she felt a little disappointed in their new employee.

Sure, he was good-looking in a tough, tanned sort of way. His clothes weren't as fancy as Brad's, who had recommended him and brought him over from the ranch in Montana. They were more workaday: thick cotton shirt, deep-blue denim jeans, tan boots with rows of stitching that showed good sturdy craftsmanship, rather than the flashy two-tones that her mom's boyfriend preferred. But it was his brash manner that was off-putting.

'You take my horse, Silver Spur,' he went on, hardly pausing to say hi to Kirstie. 'I trained that little paint from a yearling colt. Broke him and put the hours on him so that by the time he was three years old, there was no horse in Montana that could beat him for cuttin' and ropin'. He can turn on a ten cent piece and cut out any steer I choose. Why, I could almost hand the rope over to him and he'd bring in the cow all by himself!'

Brad was the last to climb into the rear seat, sandwiching Kirstie between himself and Troy. 'It's true, Silver Spur knows cows,' he confirmed. 'You'll see him in action this coming week, during spring round-up.'

Meanwhile, Matt and Sandy had taken seats in the front and Matt was easing out of the parking lot into the slow flow of traffic.

And Troy talked on. 'When I worked for Royce Morgan at Maggie Creek . . . Then there was the time with Orville Paige way out at the Padlock Ranch in Idaho . . . met up with the best horse trainers in the country . . . why those wild mustangs ain't so hard to break, not when you know how.'

All the way out on the Interstate, off along Route 3 to San Luis, through the small town and out along the Shelf-Road to Half-Moon Ranch, Kirstie listened to the big man's big talk.

And when they reached home and climbed out of the car, to be greeted by head wrangler Ben Marsh, Troy was still yakking.

He stepped out into the spring sunshine, paying no attention to the soaring mountain range behind the ranch house, nor to the fresh, free-running creek that ran through the steepsided valley. Instead, he shook hands with Ben then went straight out to look at the horses in Red Fox Meadow. 'You'll find I'm a mean judge of a quarter-horse,' he assured Ben. 'Ain't nothing about horse conformation that has me fooled, as Brad there can tell you.'

'Phew!' Sandy got out and stretched after the two-hour journey, watching Troy's receding figure. She turned with a rueful shrug to Brad. 'Is he always this mouthy?'

'Mostly,' Brad admitted. 'But the guy's genuine, believe me.'

Matt stood beside Kirstie and gazed after Troy and Ben, still able to overhear Troy putting the head wrangler right on one or two points about the shape and size of the ideal ranch horse.

'Motor-mouth, or what!' Kirstie breathed, out of hearing of her mom and Brad. She felt tired just listening.

Matt nodded and turned away. 'The Ego has landed!' he said with a grin. 'Watch this space!'

'So, Silver Spur, they tell me you're the best!' Kirstie was up with the lark next morning, helping Ben with chores in the barn. It was a Sunday and the head wrangler was preparing for a visit from a new shoer, Ray Pickett.

The boldly patterned black-and-white paint gazed sleepily at her over the fence of the adjoining pen.

'You hear me?' Kirstie insisted, pausing to lean

on her long-handled shovel and take a break from cleaning up after the horses ranged in the row-stalls, ready for the blacksmith. 'Troy says you have a great feel for rounding up those steers!'

Silver Spur blinked lazily, letting his head droop over the empty manger that separated him from Kirstie. His black forelock hung over his half-closed eyes and he flicked his white tail carelessly at the flies buzzing around in the early morning sun.

'Hmm.' Kirstie wasn't impressed. 'So what's so special?' she mused, giving Troy's horse some close attention.

True, Silver Spur had a nice head. His white muzzle was small, his nostrils good and large to suck in air at a gallop. And his brown eyes were wide set and large.

Climbing up and sitting astride the manger, Kirstie continued her study. Yep, he had a neat throat latch and his neck wasn't too chunky. There was that good forty-five degree angle from withers to shoulder that showed strength and balance. The knees were straight, the back solid and short.

Not bad, she said to herself, and she found that Silver Spur was friendly in a laid back, lazy sort of way. The horse came and nuzzled her hand and took a sniff at her shirt sleeve, probably sizing her up in the way she'd just done but in reverse.

Hmm. Young female, maybe one hundred and ten pounds, blonde hair, well put-together, knows horses. The kind of rider who won't give me any trouble.

Kirstie grinned at herself for putting thoughts into Silver Spur's head. 'OK, I'm sorry,' she told him. 'What you need right now is less of the conformation critique and more of the TLC. Wait here!'

Jumping down to the ground, she jogged down the central aisle of the cool barn past Ben, who had just led two more horses in from the meadow. 'Any sign of Troy yet?' she asked in passing.

'Nope. I gave him permission to sleep in this morning. The guy's tired after all his recent exertions and travelling.'

'So is it OK if I lead his horse into an empty stall to tidy him up?'

'Sure.' Easy-going Ben was already on the lookout for Ray Pickett so he followed Kirstie out into the yard.

She sped to the tack-room for brush, comb and hoof-pick. *Might as well give Silver Spur the full treatment*, she thought. Soon, she had him tethered in the end stall and was raising dust from his dishevelled coat.

'So, don't tell me; you're jet-lagged too,' she murmured, remembering that Silver Spur had only arrived at the ranch twenty-four hours earlier, just half a day ahead of his owner.

She and Ben had driven the trailer into San Luis yesterday morning to collect Troy's horse from the guy who'd driven him all the way down from New Jersey, where he'd been entered into a national cutting and roping contest and won third place. He'd been trailered down ahead of Troy, who'd stayed behind to judge another competition and then flown in from New York to be met at the airport by Brad and the Scotts.

So naturally the horse was tired and bored after being rattled over hundreds of miles of interstate. And sure, he still didn't look his best. But his coat was coming up nice now. It was beginning to gleam. And now that she put a steel comb to his tangled mane, it was looking silky and smooth. 'You're not bad looking after all,' she soothed.

Silver Spur blew gently through his lips – a soft, contented sound.

'Paints used to be my favourite colour, after palominos,' she confessed, warming to Silver Spur as she got to know him. 'Then I moved on to strawberry and blue roans. I like them a lot now.'

The horse snickered and flicked his ears, suddenly growing alert at the sound of a truck driving down the hill towards the ranch house.

'That's OK; it's only the new shoer,' she explained. 'Ben will be happy now he arrived.'

But Silver Spur didn't accept the explanation. His head was still up, he was shifting and stamping in the stall, rejecting Kirstie's attempts to pick out his hooves.

Soon she saw the real reason in the shape of Troy Hendren striding across the corral carrying a saddle and bridle.

'Hey, Kirstie, don't go prettying him up too good!' he called from a distance. 'I don't want him thinking he can win no beauty contest. This here guy's a working ranch-horse, pure and simple.'

Yeah, 'Thanks, Kirstie, for paying my horse some attention!' she thought. Then she stepped aside to let the cowboy saddle up.

'You riding out with us?' Troy inquired, slapping the saddle over Silver Spur's broad back, fastening the cinch and straightening the heavy stirrups.

'Where are you planning on going?'

'Along the creek. We might find us a couple of cows in those willows I caught sight of when we drove in.'

'Yeah, sure I'll ride.' Kirstie was never one to turn down an invitation. 'We'd better leave some cows out there for next week's guests, though. They jet in from all over the country just to play cowboy and round up those steers!'

Easing the metal bit between Silver Spur's lips, Troy grinned. 'OK, we'll leave a couple for them,' he agreed.

So Kirstie hurried to fetch Lucky from Red Fox Meadow and saddle him. Eager as ever, the palomino stood patiently while he was tacked up.

'. . . Yeah, good idea.' Ben was talking with Troy as she worked. 'You ride out with Kirstie. She can show you some of the trails we use, like Five Mile Creek Trail and Bear Hunt Trail. It's gonna take you a couple of weeks to learn the ropes around here, so the sooner you start the better.'

Troy nodded quietly. 'You're the boss.'

'Ready!' Kirstie called.

'Seven-thirty. Give yourselves two hours, be back for nine-thirty,' Ben suggested. He stood alongside the short, burly figure of Ray Pickett who was dressed in jeans, white vest and leather apron, his dark moustache drooping over an unsmiling mouth.

'That guy had muscles where I didn't know I had places!' Troy joked as he led the way out of the corral. 'What is it about shoers that they all look like Burt Reynolds in that buddy movie from way back?'

Kirstie missed the reference but appreciated Troy's style. As with his horse, the man seemed to improve after you got to know him a little. Like, she'd seen him give Ben the respect he deserved as head wrangler, so any worry that his brash manner might overpower quiet Ben was probably groundless. And he really did ride well.

More than well. He sat in the saddle like a natural, weight centred, back straight, moving with the horse's gait as if he and the horse were part of the same organism. And his hands were light. He put no visible pressure on the reins to get Silver Spur moving this way or that. What's more, though he wore a showy pair of gleaming spurs, he only had to touch his horse's flanks and shift his weight to achieve a change of gait, from walk to trot then trot to lope, in one smooth movement.

So Brad had been right about that when he recommended Troy as one of the best riders he'd seen in his entire life. 'Give the guy a break,' he'd pleaded with Sandy. 'He had a tough time on his last ranch and parted company on a point of principle. Troy didn't like the way his boss acted with the horses in the ramuda. One day he told him so and the guy turned and socked him in the jaw with the spade he had in his hand.

'Troy landed in the local hospital with a busted face, and meanwhile his boss blackened his name up and down the county. Said he was gonna make sure Troy never got another job rounding up steers as long as he lived.'

The account had worked with Sandy Scott, who said she trusted Brad's judgment. And since Charlie's decision to leave Half-Moon Ranch had been a spur of the moment thing, dependent on the college term, she was hard pushed to get a replacement in time for the spring round-up.

Which was how come Kirstie and Lucky were following Troy and Silver Spur along the green bank of Five Mile Creek early on a Sunday morning in late April.

'Pretty,' Troy observed, glancing up at Eagle's Peak, still covered in winter snow. 'It reminds me of my time in south-west Colorado, down New Mexico way. One time, I was working cattle at an outpost on a big spread and I didn't see a single human being for weeks on end. Just beefs. A thousand head, up in them hills, all above ten thousand feet. And I had to get them all down before the first snow set in. Man, that was a lot of cows!'

'Just as well we've only got a couple of hundred,' Kirstie remarked. 'The way our dude riders behave around cattle, we're lucky to bring in twenty per day!'

'Yeah, right!' Laughing, Troy pulled Silver Spur to a sudden stop. He'd spotted what they'd come out looking for: a lone cow with her spring calf quietly grazing the lush grass on the bank of the creek about two hundred yards ahead.

Eventually, Kirstie picked them out too. She saw that between them and their quarry was a stretch of tall willow bushes through which the clear water trickled and swirled. The creek was shallow enough, but scattered with rocks and boulders; by no means an easy approach.

Even now, at this distance, the nursing mother had raised her heavy white head and registered their presence. She motioned the young calf closer to her side.

'So much for stealin' up on 'em nice and quiet,' Troy muttered. Then he issued a sharp order to Kirstie. 'You and Lucky take this side of the creek. Your aim is to head them out of the willows into that draw on the left. My job is to cross the creek, lope along the far bank and charge back through the water to scare them into stampeding off in your direction. OK?'

Kirstie nodded. She felt Lucky's muscles bunch up.

And beside her, Silver Spur was suddenly a new horse. Gone was the sleepy look, the downbeat style. In their place was a super-alert stance, ears pricked forward, neck arched, eyes boring into the distant target.

'Ready?' Troy whispered.

Another nod. Kirstie sat tight in the saddle and squeezed Lucky's sides.

They were off, weaving through the bushes.

'Yee-hah!' Troy set up the cowboy cry.

He guided Silver Spur into the middle of the creek, urged him into a lope and began to surge through the water in a burst of sun-spangled spray.

2

Through the creek, up the far bank, Silver Spur thundered towards the startled steer and her calf.

Kirstie felt the adrenalin rush as she met the challenge of weaving neatly through the willows, ducking, bending to this side then that, as Troy and his horse went full gallop out of the water. She watched Silver Spur leap a rock in his path and swerve around the broad trunk of a pine tree just beyond, marvelling at how Troy managed to keep his balance at the same time as unhitching a coil of rope from around the saddle horn.

Meanwhile, the two frightened creatures set up a

bellow and a bleat that could be heard all down the valley.

'Yee-hah!' Troy yelled again. He began to swing his lasso around his head as he rode full-gallop.

By this time, Kirstie and Lucky had drawn level with the gulley down which they hoped to trap the cows. So she pulled on the reins and sat way back in the saddle to stop Lucky and wait in the appointed position.

And Troy had raced along the bank to a point where he chose to steer Silver Spur back through the water and scare the cows into blundering towards Kirstie. The paint changed direction in mid stride; a flying lead-change like none she'd ever seen. Practically superhuman riding. The horse plunged into the creek, kicking up spray, determined to drive the cattle towards the draw.

'Clever!' Kirstie approved of the paint horse's unerring instinct.

The poor steer bellowed, rushing ahead of her calf away from the charging horse. The youngster bleated feebly and followed on still-wobbly legs.

'They're heading this way!' Kirstie warned Lucky. 'We stand firm, OK!'

Her palomino didn't flinch as fifteen hundred pounds of muscle and bone pounded through the willows towards him. Branches were trampled and crushed, or sprang back like whips. Mud sucked at the cow and calf's cloven hooves, slowing them down so that Lucky and Kirstie were able to inch forward and divert them sideways down the draw.

'Good job!' Troy yelled, lasso still circling. 'Yee-hah!' He flipped the rope with an expert twist of the wrist, leaning sideways from the saddle as Silver Spur thundered out of the creek and into the gulley.

The mother cow came to the dead end they'd planned, turned and dipped her shoulders in panic. Thrown off balance, she was an easy target for the snaking loop of rope.

Kirstie heard it whistle through the still air, saw it land fair and square over the black steer's head, watched Troy sit back in the saddle and pull tight.

His job done, the paint horse stopped in an instant. Front legs braced, back ones bent and haunches tucked under, he slid to a halt.

'Yeah!' Troy crowed, fastening the rope tight around the saddle horn.

'Cool!' Kirstie could see that the cowboy might have made a lot of noise and given the appearance of being a flashy show-off, but that really he'd used minimum effort and force. She was glad about this, disliking as she did the idea that the unlucky cow might get hurt in this kind of manoeuvre.

And she knew enough to realise that the pathetic wails of the young calf would soon stop and that he would quietly follow his mother as soon as Troy released her from the noose and Silver Spur herded her firmly back to the ranch.

Sure enough, the half-mile ride back home went smoothly, since the fight had gone out of the cow. Less than half an hour after she and Troy had set out, they arrived in triumph with the first steers of the spring round-up.

'You should've see them!' Kirstie wanted to relive the moment with Hadley Crane, the retired head wrangler who still lived with the Scotts at Half-Moon Ranch.

She'd found him after breakfast that same morning, leaning idly on the corral fence, watching Ben and the shoer at work. The old man never let his reactions show on his lined face or emerge in his tone of voice, which was always flat and expressionless.

'Really, Hadley; Troy is good!'

'I never saw him, but I sure heard him,' he commented. 'Anyone between here and San Luis probably heard him too.'

Kirstie had seen Hadley rope enough cattle himself to know that not so much as a whisper passed his lips as he worked. Hadley was more the traditional strong, silent type. So she decided to switch tack. 'OK, then. How about Silver Spur? If I told you that the horse is the best cutting and roping horse I ever saw outside the competition arena in Denver, would you believe me?'

There was silence except for the metallic tap-tap-tap of Ray Pickett's hammer as he fitted new shoes on old Crazy Horse. Bent over, the giant hoof cupped in his broad hand and using his crooked leg as a support, the shoer flexed his biceps and hammered away.

'Yeah, I know the horse is good,' Hadley agreed. 'He got third in New Jersey. Guys I know say he'll move up a place in Dallas next month. By the end of the season, he'll be taking first prize.'

'You should see his balance and speed!' Kirstie waxed lyrical. She was a recent Silver Spur convert and wanted to share her discovery with anyone who would stand still long enough to listen. 'He's made real neat. Not an ounce of spare flesh; just solid muscle. And to think, first time I looked at him I thought he was just some plain, sleepy old, ordinary quarter-horse!'

'Hmm.' The old man's gaze followed the shoer as he handed Crazy Horse over to Ben, who led him back into his stall. Then he picked up his tall grey stetson from the fence post and fixed it firmly on his head. 'Nope,' he contradicted. 'You were wrong there. Ain't nothing plain or ordinary about that little guy . . . It's just a pity about his owner, that's all.'

'Give Troy a chance is all I ask!' Sandy Scott pleaded over breakfast next morning.

It was thirty minutes before Kirstie was due to set out for school, and the old man had once more expressed his doubts about the new wrangler.

'All I'm saying is, that guy can't really have done even half of what he claims.' Hadley refused to back down from his poor opinion of Troy. 'Why, he's worked on so many top ranches and won so many contests, I need a whole book to write 'em all down!'

Kirstie smiled. She knew what Hadley was getting at when she remembered the wrangler's behaviour from last evening.

This was when a bunch of new guests had got to meet the ranch staff at the routine Sunday evening get-together by the corral fence.

'Has everyone been assigned a horse for the

week?' Ben had checked. Carrying out this introductory part of his role as boss-man on staff was his least favourite part of the job. But he carried it out with a certain jokey style which Kirstie always liked.

The recent arrivals had all nodded.

'Has Troy here fitted you all for saddles?' he'd continued.

A dark-haired woman and her teenaged daughter had gone over, there and then, to be measured up. Troy had made them giggle in embarrassment with a couple of innuendoes about their weight, delivered in a deadpan undertone.

'And have y'all read this notice which we have fixed to the side of the tack-room here, drawing your attention to the fact that in the event of injury or death, Colorado State law puts responsibility with the rider, not the ranch?'

Kirstie recalled the uneasy silence, which Ben had filled with a wry aside. ''Course, we always aim to keep deaths to a minimum here at Half-Moon Ranch.'

Small, sheepish grins had broken out amongst the guests. Then Ben had handed them over to Troy, who was to give them special pointers to help their riding during round-up week.

'Now, I don't know how y'all like to eat your steak.' Troy had begun in a roundabout way. He'd sat astride the fence, long legs hitched up on to a lower rail, jeans neatly starched and pressed in true cowboy fashion. 'Personally, I like to take the cow, clean it up a little, show it the flame and slap it on the plate!'

'Yuck!' The girl who'd recently had her saddle fitting had spoken out.

The rest of the guests had laughed.

And that had set Troy off on a roll, describing the faintheartedness of many consumers who never made the direct connection between the animals out on the range and the food they stored in their freezers. He'd teased and joked his way through the introductory session, swaggering a little, playing up his cowboy past. 'Now I broke just about every bone in my body since I began,' he'd warned them. Tough guy Troy. 'The fact is, if you come off your horse, you just gotta get straight back on him and cowboy up!'

'Yeah!' The guys in the visiting group had agreed, while the women had looked nervous.

It had been necessary for Ben to step back in then and reassure everyone that Half-Moon Ranch's safety record was in fact good. 'You pay no mind to

Troy's macho stuff,' he'd told Alicia Rankin, the dark-haired guest's anxious, thin-skinned daughter. 'He's new here, so he's still a little too mouthy!'

The guests had enjoyed laughing at Troy's expense and Troy himself had taken the comment in good spirit.

But now Hadley had passed a remark at breakfast to the effect that the newcomer was a reckless show-off and needed to be watched closely before Sandy let him loose on the trail with a bunch of novice riders.

Kirstie's mom defended her choice, but the old man hung on in. 'Take yesterday morning,' he insisted. 'Not only does the guy go out lookin' for cows when what he should be doin' is learnin' the trails, but what else does he do? He only ropes a steer that's up against a dead-end draw. Where's the sense in that, since the cow wasn't going nowhere whether he roped her or not!'

'OK, I agree that Troy's a handful,' Sandy conceded.

It was time for Kirstie to gather her school things and set off with Matt for town. But not before she'd seen Hadley jam his hat down on his head and deliver his parting shot.

'Call me a misery guts,' he declared, 'but if Troy

Hendren has worked every place he says he's worked and done everything he claims to have done in every state between here and the Mexican border, why that guy would be dang near a hundred years old!'

Hadley was in a minority of one, it seemed.

Kirstie had spent the day in school and come back home half expecting to find that the old wrangler's poor opinion of Troy had spread.

But no; what did she see when she stepped out of Sandy's car and looked across the yard to the arena? Only the man himself and Silver Spur thrilling the guests with an impromptu display of horsemanship.

'Wow!' a kid from Idaho gasped as Troy brought his paint to a spectacular sliding stop. His back heels raised dust in a cloud that drifted towards the spectators.

'That's nothin',' Troy boasted. 'Just watch him spin!'

Nudging Silver Spur with his left knee and neck reining him to the right, the cowboy set his horse into a rapid pirouette turn on his back legs. The front feet crossed rapidly, dainty as a ballerina, while the back feet stayed glued to the spot. Round and round they went, allowing another loud gasp to build up amongst the visitors.

'Jeez, he really can turn on a dime!' A guest from New York State sang Silver Spur's praises. 'I caught him taking third prize in the national cutting championship last week, and I can tell you that horse is world class!'

'Think of all the work that went into it.' Joe Stefan, the boy from Idaho, tried to get his head round the level of skill on display in the arena. 'Y'know, I was talking with Troy out on the trail today, and he told me they put in three hours' training per day to reach this standard.'

'How could he find the time to do three hours every day if he was working on a ranch in my home state like he said?' Alicia Rankin wondered.

Standing beside her, her mother nodded. 'Yeah, that doesn't stack up,' she agreed.

Brad was visiting Sandy for the afternoon and had been helping bring horses in from the meadow to be shoed by Ray Pickett on his second day at the ranch. He was close enough to overhear the mother and daughter cast doubt. 'You folks are from Montana, huh?'

Linda Rankin, the mother, nodded again. She was a homely sort of woman, a little overweight, who seemed nervous around horses and who had come

28

on a ranching vacation mostly for her daughter's sake. 'We're from Butte, way out west.'

'OK, well Troy worked in the south of the state, just outside Billings, north of the Crow Indian reservation. And the work he did for Red Owen on the Triple R was horse breaking and training, not straight cowboying. His job was to bring on the colts and two-year-olds. And part of the deal was that Troy got to train his own cutting horse too.'

'Well, he did a pretty good job,' Joe Stefan concluded generously. He was a cute-faced, blond kid of about eleven with a turned-up nose and an easy, friendly manner.

'You bet!' a bank manager named Mike Nicholls added, as Troy demonstrated flying lead-changes across the arena.

And everyone else in the crowd of about a dozen agreed.

Except down-in-the-mouth Linda Rankin, who, it seemed to Kirstie, had grown determined to pick fault. 'You say Troy worked for a guy named Red Owen?' she checked with Brad.

Frowning slightly, he grunted, 'Yeah. Why?'

'Nothin'. Only, I have a cousin, Kirk, on my late husband's side of the family who works in Billings. I seem to remember hearing there'd been trouble at the Triple R late last fall. I don't recall any of the details; just that it made the local papers . . .'

'Wowee!' Joe cut across Linda Rankin's wandering thoughts with another yelp of delight as Troy made Silver Spur slide to a stop only twelve inches from the fence where they all stood.

The showman took off his stetson and bowed to the crowd, who applauded loudly.

But Kirstie's mind was no longer on the spectacular demonstration. Instead, she was staring into Brad's face.

It was as if a cloud had passed over it. No more smiles, no more easy chat. At Linda Rankin's mention of her cousin in Billings, a knot had appeared between his brows. He'd given a small shake of his head and turned away even while the woman was speaking. 'I got work to do,' he muttered before walking quickly away.

'Now what type of incident was it that Kirk described to us?' Linda Rankin was saying to herself, since there was nobody to listen to her meanderings now that Brad had cut her dead. 'If I recall correctly, someone got hurt. And something else after that. Rumours about money going missing maybe . . .'

She paused, her broad face creased into a frown, until she finally let the subject drop. 'No, I forget,' she sighed. 'Of course, I had a lot on my mind back then. And anyway, I guess it couldn't have been anything real important . . .'

3

'Did you hear? We brought in fifteen cows today!' Joe Stefan announced to Kirstie proudly on the Tuesday evening. 'That makes a total of seventy-eight for the week so far. Not bad, huh?'

Kirstie had joined the guests after school for an evening cook-out by Five Mile Creek. It had been a hot day, with the temperature touching eighty – a forerunner of the short, dry summer to come. In any case, she was glad of a cooler breeze now, and the chance to dip her feet in the crystal water. Across the stream, the ranch's hardworking horses ate contentedly in Red Fox Meadow.

Rodeo Rocky, Hollywood Princess, Johnny Mohawk – she picked out the athletic bay, the glamorous American Albino and her constant companion, the little black stallion.

'Fifteen cows!' Joe repeated, pressing for a reaction. 'That was just me on Jitterbug and Troy on Silver Spur. Two of us brought down the whole fifteen from Eden Lake without any help.'

'Good job,' Kirstie murmured, sighing at the effect of the cool water on her tired feet. 'Jitterbug can be a handful around cows. You did well.'

'We found 'em in a pass east of Crystal Creek.' There was no stopping Joe now that he'd started. 'Snowmelt had swelled the stream and cut the steers off from the lower pastures. Pretty soon they'd have run out of grass if we hadn't shown up.'

'So did you have to drive them back across the creek?' Kirstie pictured the difficult task. Crystal Creek ran into Eden Lake over a steep fall. When the stream was swollen, it was easily possible for either horses or cattle to lose their footing and be swept over the edge.

Joe nodded, enjoying the fact that he was gathering an audience. Two sisters from Arizona, Tessa and Hayley Eastmann, had wandered along the bank to listen. Dressed in bright pink and yellow

T-shirts and denim shorts, they came armed with plates of hamburgers, corn chips and salad.

'The water was way past Jitterbug's belly,' he told Kirstie, 'but she cowboyed up and went ahead when she saw Silver Spur take the creek in his stride. The tricky bit was driving the steers back with us. We had five calves in the bunch, and they sure didn't like the pull of that current.'

'But you made it.' Kirstie was impressed.

The blond guest nodded. 'Yeah, and guess what, I get to help Troy brand the calves after the cook-out.'

'Can we watch?' Hayley asked eagerly. She and her younger sister obviously liked to be part of the action. They'd seemed a bit envious as they'd listened to Joe's exciting account.

'We're gonna ask Ben if we can ride out with Troy tomorrow,' Tessa told him. She was a small girl of about nine, with a heavy, dark fringe and a gappy grin. 'Guys who ride out with Troy always have the most fun!'

'He sure is a joker,' Joe confirmed, glancing across the cook-out area to where the new wrangler was fooling around as usual with his lasso.

'Alicia, don't move!' Troy cried, swinging the rope around his head.

Linda Rankin's daughter sat isolated from the happy-go-lucky crowd, her head buried in a book. She glanced up moodily when Troy attracted her attention.

'Uh-oh!' Kirstie could see that Alicia wasn't going to appreciate this.

Troy rotated his wrist and let go of the rope. It flew across the ten-yard gap and looped neatly around Alicia's head and shoulders. 'Yee-hah!'

'Yeah!' Joe yelled his approval. 'Neat throw, Troy!'

'Very funny!' Alicia blushed bright red, her round face creased by a frown. 'Now would you please get this thing off of me.'

Hayley grinned. 'Alicia needs to chill out a little, don't you think?'

By this time Troy was obligingly freeing his prisoner. 'How about I teach you to rope?'

The sullen girl shook her head. 'No thanks. But since you're here, I can tell you I need a new horse tomorrow.'

'You do?' Troy raised an eyebrow. 'What's wrong with the horse you've got?'

'It's Yukon,' Alicia said in a tone of disgust, as if that explained everything.

'So?'

'She's too slow. I want a peppy horse – something

like Jitterbug or Rodeo Rocky.'

'Yukon has plenty of pep,' Troy contradicted. 'It's a question of how you handle her, that's all.'

'No way. She's old and slow and ornery,' Alicia insisted. 'She keeps wanting to eat out on the trail. And she doesn't like chasing cows.'

'Hmm.'

Kirstie read volumes into Troy's studied silence. She guessed that Alicia Rankin was one of those nightmare guests who thought they were much better riders than they actually were. Ben would have chosen Yukon for her precisely because the brown-and-white paint horse had a steady, patient temper and could put up with a novice in the saddle.

'And another thing, I want to ride in your group tomorrow,' Alicia declared. Like her mom, she was short and solid with straight brown hair which she allowed to hang forward over her face. 'I don't see why Joe gets to ride with you two days running and the rest of us don't get a choice.'

'Yeah.' Troy shrugged non-commitally. 'I guess you need to work that out with Ben.'

So the girl stood up, ready to seek out the head wrangler and repeat her demands. But as she was looking for him among the twenty or so guests, she caught sight of her mother hurrying along the side of the creek towards them.

'Hey, what kept you?' Alicia said accusingly. 'I'm hungry. C'mon, let's eat!'

'Yeah, honey, soon.' Linda Rankin looked about her distractedly. She spied Kirstie sitting by the creek with Joe, Hayley and Tessa and went quickly to join them.

'Have you seen your mom?' Linda asked Kirstie.

'Sure. She's over there behind the barbie.' Kirstie had the feeling that now wasn't the time for Linda Rankin to bother her mom about some small detail to do with towels in their cabin or some such. Sandy already had her hands full serving burgers to a bunch of ravenous guests. 'Can I help?' she offered instead.

'Yeah – no – I don't know!' Alicia's mom seemed upset. She kept putting a hand to her throat and stroking her skin. 'I went back to my cabin to find my locket, but it's not there.'

Kirstie frowned. 'What kind of locket?'

'Antique gold. I turned the whole place upside down . . . Alicia, you know the one I mean?'

Her daughter nodded. 'It's the one with Dad's picture in.'

'Yeah, that one. I can't have lost it. I'm always so careful . . .'

'What does it look like exactly?' Kirstie was picking up the message that the missing piece of jewellery had high sentimental value.

'It's oval, about this big.' Linda made the shape with her thumb and forefinger. 'On a heavy gold chain. The photograph is the last one I took of RW before he died last fall.'

'Gee, I'm sorry.' Kirstie was still hopeful that Linda Rankin had simply mislaid her necklace. 'Would you like me to help you look again?' she suggested.

So Kirstie, Alicia and Linda left the cook-out and took the track up past Brown Bear Cabin where Hadley stayed, to the first of four new cabins built to cope with the extra guests that Half-Moon Ranch was beginning to attract. The Rankins' cabin was called Hummingbird and was set back from the path in the shade of a pinewood copse.

Inside, Kirstie saw that everything was precisely in its place; the lamps, the magazines on the desk, the coffee-making machine all looked untouched. And in the bedroom, behind the living-room, she found that the Rankins' passion for tidiness continued. The bed was neatly made, there wasn't a stray T-shirt or even a sock in sight.

'I keep the locket in this small wooden casket.' Linda picked up the box from the bedside cabinet and opened it to show Kirstie the empty interior. 'I don't wear it to ride, in case I lose it. Normally, I come back, take a shower, get dressed and put on the necklace before dinner. But when I came to do that half an hour ago, I found it had gone!'

'And you're sure you couldn't have put it some place else?' Kirstie encouraged Linda to look again. But there was such order about the way these two lived that she was beginning to think it was unlikely that Linda would have been careless with something so precious.

And she felt sad for them, having lost 'RW' so recently. Perhaps this vacation had been Linda's way of helping Alicia to get over the death of her father. If so, it had begun to go badly wrong.

'It's not here!' Linda sighed, having searched again.

'Well come on, let's go back and tell Mom,' Kirstie decided.

'Yeah, and I need to eat,' Alicia put in, marching back down the hill towards the creek.

Great! Kirstie hoped she wouldn't behave so badly if something like this happened to her mom. By now she felt Linda was on the verge of tears and ready to blame anyone or anything that came her way.

'I don't know why you people don't put locks on these cabin doors,' she complained. 'When I first arrived, I said to Alicia that I didn't feel safe without a key. It's all very well you telling guests that there's no crime around here, but now look what happened!'

'Listen, I'm sure there's some explanation,' Kirstie said hurriedly, heading straight for her mom who by now had finished serving food. She wanted to deal with the situation quietly and hopefully get Sandy to quiz Linda once more about when and where she last saw the locket.

But Mrs Rankin wasn't the type to be discreet. Instead, she pushed her way between guests sitting at bench-tables with the remains of their meals and spoke to Sandy in a loud, theatrical voice. 'I had a gut feeling that something bad would happen before the week was through,' she announced gloomily. 'And, sure enough, my gold locket has gone from its casket!'

The news sent an uneasy ripple through the other guests. Sandy took off her apron and Ben and Hadley approached from the wooden footbridge

over the creek. Troy was the only member of the ranch staff to ignore the growing kerfuffle and carry on joking with the two Eastmann girls.

'Mrs Rankin, are you sure?' Sandy asked in a worried voice.

'Sure I'm sure. Ask Kirstie. She just came with me to take a second look.' By now, it was as if the world had ended. Tears had welled up and Linda's voice had grown jerky and cracked. 'That locket has been in my family for generations. And then there's the picture of RW, which can never be replaced. It'll break my heart if it's gone.'

Sandy flashed Kirstie a worried look, then tried to reach out a comforting hand to Linda Rankin. 'Let's just try to think what can have happened here.'

But the distressed woman pulled away. 'We know what's happened!' she insisted. It seemed to Kirstie that she was playing to the crowd, raising her tearful voice and demanding attention. 'What's happened is that a thief walked right into my cabin and stole my gold locket!'

'Thirty-five calves, thirty-five nursing mothers, which makes a total of seventy, leaving eight cows without calves!' Troy called out the grand total from the count they'd just made.

Ben nodded and made a mental note. Then he planned ahead. 'Which leaves us one hundred and twenty-two head to bring in before the weekend. Troy, I'd like you to ride out to Dorfmann Lake tomorrow. It's a favourite spot in the spring, three miles upstream from here. We usually bring plenty in from there.'

Keeping Silver Spur to a slow trot, Troy made a careful circuit around the outside of the big holding-pen where the cattle jostled and bellowed. He looked in with an expert eye, selecting out the eight mature cows which had failed to produce calves and getting ready to go in there and cut them out.

'We need to bring in the vet to look at them,' Ben explained to Joe Stefan, who stood nearby holding Jitterbug on a lead-rope. 'It's most likely that those cows aborted their calves and it'd be good to find out the reason why.'

'So what happens now exactly?' Tessa Eastmann wanted to know. She coughed at the dust raised by the cattle in the pen, then ducked back to stand with Kirstie under the shelter of the overhanging barn roof.

'Troy and Silver Spur cut out the eight, then drive them down that shute at the far end of the pen into the small area by the creek,' Kirstie explained. She knew from experience to stand upwind of a bunch of unhappy cows, out of line of the dust cloud raised by their shuffling hooves. 'Joe and Jitterbug will help them along. We hold them overnight and Glen Woodford drives in from San Luis early tomorrow to take samples and do blood tests.'

'When do we get to watch the babies being freeze-branded?' Hayley chipped in. 'Will that be tonight, before it gets dark?'

'No, that'll be tomorrow. We need Ray Pickett to come along again, with his gas canister.' Kirstie had seen the shoer drive away in his pick-up during the time when the whole ranch was busy searching for Linda Rankin's lost locket. 'In the old days of hot-branding, when Grandpa had the ranch, he could heat the irons in the furnace and do the job himself. These days, it needs special equipment.'

Branding was one of the useful services offered by the new blacksmith and a reason why Ben had chosen him after Chuck Perry had moved away to live near Durango.

That evening, Ray had hung around talking to Troy while the case of the missing locket had been investigated. Kirstie had passed them by in the yard and overheard them shrugging their shoulders about 'neurotic lady guests'.

'She's the type who breaks a fingernail and considers it a major tragedy,' Troy had confided in the blacksmith with evident lack of sympathy.

Eventually, Ray had grown tired of waiting for Ben to show up and help Troy cut out the thirty calves for branding. So he'd gone home, promising to be back first thing the next day.

'Ready?' Troy called across to Joe, who quickly jumped into the saddle. 'When I go in and cut out the first steer, I need you to be standing by the gate. The moment I drive her through, you cut across the exit on Jitterbug and discourage the rest of the herd from stampeding after her.'

'Yessir!' A nervous dude rider got ready to carry out the order.

Kirstie, Tessa and Hayley watched quietly as Troy entered the holding-pen. He rode Silver Spur into the dusty mêlée, focusing on the calfless cow which he'd selected as his first customer. The broad-backed cattle parted at the approach of the horse and rider, barging into each other in their crowded efforts to get out of their path.

'Silver Spur is great, isn't he?' Hayley breathed. 'He goes right in and shows those cows who's the boss!'

The black-and-white paint was working well, understanding his task. He too seemed to know which cow had been chosen, heading straight towards it without noticing the heaving mass of cattle to either side. Kirstie grinned in approval. That sure was one skilful, expert cow-horse.

And soon Troy and Silver Spur had isolated the steer – which had a distinctive black patch of hair over her right eye. They worked her along the fence, pushing her steadily towards the exit where Joe and Jitterbug stood ready. And though the cow resisted, the team soon had her through the gate and into the shute which led to the smaller creekside pen.

'Yee-hah!' Troy gave a triumphant cry and gave Joe a high-five as he rode by to cut out the second cow.

Joe Stefan beamed, sitting straight in the saddle, seemingly having grown a whole two inches since supper.

'I gotta go,' Kirstie told the Eastmann girls. She'd spotted Linda Rankin hurrying down from Hummingbird to accost her mom on the ranch-house porch.

Maybe the locket turned up, she thought brightly, running alongside the barn and across the yard to find out.

But no: her mom's face was serious as she listened to Mrs Rankin talk. She said nothing in reply, just stood and took in what the guest had to say.

'I called my cousin Kirk, in Billings,' Linda announced, hands clenched to her chest in a state of nervous excitement. 'There was something at the back of my mind that had been bugging me ever since I heard Brad Martin say that Troy Hendren worked for Red Owen on the Three Rs.'

Drawing close, Kirstie slowed down. This sounded like the sort of news she didn't want to hear.

Linda Rankin rushed to deliver it with told-you-so intensity. 'Kirk said, yeah there was trouble at Owen's place last year. It involved a trainer he employed called, guess what – Troy Hendren!'

'Sure, I know all about that,' Sandy insisted. 'It was a fight over the way Red Owen wanted his horses trained. Troy landed in hospital with a broken jaw.'

Linda frowned and shook her head. 'Not the way I heard it. I just got Kirk to remind me what really happened. He told me the bust-up wasn't over no horse, it was about an antique rifle Red had hanging over his fireplace. It was a real pretty piece, worth a couple of thousand dollars, belonging to Red's great-grandfather way back.'

Kirstie saw her mom close her eyes and take a deep breath. They both knew what was coming next.

And sure enough, Linda Rankin delivered the final blow. 'The fact is, Red Owen socked Troy Hendren in the jaw because he found his great-grandpa's rifle stashed away under Troy's bunk. The guy's an out-and-out thief, Sandy. And unless I'm totally mistaken, he's the one who stole my locket!'

4

Kirstie woke next morning to the sound of calves wailing from the holding-pen by Five Mile Creek.

Groaning, with only one eye half-open she studied the clock on her bedside table.

Five-thirty! A time when no civilised person should even contemplate getting up. The dawn light was still dull and grey through her open window, the blue jays in the pine trees at the back of the house only just starting to call.

But Kirstie could tell from the noise the calves were making that the wranglers were already at work, cutting out the thirty-five youngsters from their mothers, ready for Ray Pickett to begin branding when he arrived. The poor things cried pitifully, while the full-grown steers bellowed out their own deep protests.

Kirstie knew she might as well kiss goodbye to any more sleep. So reluctantly she pushed back her sheets and stumbled for the work clothes she'd left slung over the back of a chair. With more than two hours in hand before she needed to set out for school, she figured she might as well go down and give the guys a hand.

Still bleary-eyed, she groped her way into her jeans and shirt, took her boots in her hand and crept quietly downstairs so as not to wake her mom and Matt.

Long after Kirstie had gone to bed, the two of them had stayed up, discussing Linda Rankin's accusation against Troy.

'We have two versions of what happened at the Triple R,' Sandy had pointed out, having calmed the distressed guest and taken her safely back to her cabin. 'One is the stolen-rifle-under-the-bunk story, which Linda Rankin's cousin just passed on. The other is Brad's account, which sets Troy in a whole lot better light.'

'So the question is: which one do we believe?' Matt had tried to stay reasonable for Sandy's sake. Left to himself, Kirstie figured that her hothead brother would probably have acted right away, splashing out with the accusations to judge Troy's response.

From her warm bed, Kirstie had listened to the long silence that her mom had allowed to develop. There was a lot at stake, not only Troy's reputation but the name of Half-Moon Ranch. If it got around that they employed dubious wranglers and that valuable objects went missing from guests' cabins, reservations would definitely take a sudden and steep dive.

'As far as I can make out, there was never any proof that the rifle incident actually took place,' Sandy had said at last. 'Even Linda admits that there was no court case, no conviction . . .'

'Only rumour.' Matt had waited for Sandy to make up her mind.

'The thing is, can there be smoke without fire?' Their mom had thought her way all around the problem. 'On the other hand, I trust Brad's word. Which means this whole thing could've been set up by Red Owen as a smokescreen for the bad way he treats his horses . . .'

Another silence, broken by Matt. 'Leave it for now, huh, Mom?'

'Yeah. At least I persuaded Linda Rankin not to shoot her mouth off until I'd double-checked the facts.'

Kirstie had heard chairs scrape over the kitchen floor as her mom and brother had got up to go to bed.

'First thing tomorrow morning I'll ask Hadley if he has any contacts close to Billings. That way, maybe we'll get an independent account of what really went on.' Sandy's decision had been cautious and considered.

But Kirstie had overheard Matt's final warning remark as he trailed sleepily upstairs. 'Meanwhile, we have to admit that we've got a thief on the ranch,' he'd reminded his mom. 'And we've gotta move pretty darned fast to stop this happening again!'

Maybe that tense conversation was one reason, along with the crying calves, why Kirstie had woken so early and failed to get back to sleep. Her head was still buzzing with the problem as she stepped out on to the porch, put on her boots and crossed the yard.

'How many calves do we have now?' Ben called

from the holding-pen, where the grown cows shunted into one another and pressed against the sturdy fence rails. Riding Crazy Horse amongst them, the head wrangler's head and shoulders bobbed above the flat black backs of the anxious steers.

'Twenty-eight,' Troy answered from the smaller pen by the creek.

Kirstie made out that the guys had already separated most of the calves and held them with the eight infertile cows. Naturally, the youngsters were kicking up a fuss, straining to make their way back up the narrow shute to be with their mothers.

But Troy had the situation under control. He and Silver Spur totally looked the part: Troy in his black work stetson and cream checked shirt, Silver Spur gutsy and determined as he blocked the calves' return route.

'OK, Kirstie, we need to cut seven more calves out from this bunch.' Spying extra help, Ben rode to the fence.

'Do I have time to fetch Lucky and saddle him up?'

'Nope,' Troy cut in as he closed the interlinking gate and rode Silver Spur up the shute. 'Here, you take my horse. I can work on foot from here on in.'

'Really?' Kirstie knew it was a big thing for a cowboy to give up his horse to another rider.

But Troy downplayed it. 'Sure. Take a turn on the expert!' he offered, swinging down from the saddle and handing over the reins. And before she knew it he was returning to his position in the lower pen. 'Push those babies down to me!' he yelled cheerfully. 'Then we can all go cook us some grits and bacon for breakfast!'

Up in the saddle, Kirstie got to learn what riding a real professional cow-horse was all about.

'I could've sat there doing nothing and Silver Spur would still have cut out those calves all by himself,' she said later to her mom and Matt.

Which wasn't quite true. But all he needed was the gentlest touch to set him going after each of the seven youngsters. Kirstie would shift her weight slightly in the saddle and Silver Spur would turn. She would click her tongue and he would pick up speed, pull gently on the reins and he would stop to give the calf room to point itself down the shute.

And there Troy would be, to open the gate and urge the calf along.

'The real test of a horse comes when something goes wrong,' she asserted over breakfast. 'Take the time when one of the calves slipped right under the fence rail and escaped into the creek.'

'How did that happen?' Matt wanted to know.

'He charged the fence and butted the rail. It gave way and he made his break.' Kirstie enjoyed telling the tale.

'Silver Spur sees this little guy making his bid for freedom. He's after him like a bullet, without me telling him. Wow, that horse can sure move. We're down the shute, flying at the fence, and we're clean over it before I catch my breath. Then we're crashing through the water after the calf, and Silver Spur gets into the right position to head him off. I tell you, there was only the horse and me between him and the whole of the Rocky Mountains!'

Matt and Sandy grinned. 'How did you get him back?' Matt asked. 'Did you rope him like a real cowboy?'

'Nope. Troy did that bit,' she admitted. 'He ran through the creek fully dressed and tossed the lasso over the runaway's head, neat as you like. Then I got to take the end of the rope and tie it around Silver Spur's saddle horn. Between us we got him back in that pen and Ben had already shored up the broken fence, no problem.'

As she paused for breath and to tuck into her

waffle before it went cold, Sandy crept in with the topic that was worrying them all. 'And Troy's OK?' she asked Kirstie quietly. 'He didn't seem upset or anything?'

Kirstie looked up from her plate with a slight shake of her head. 'You mean, upset by this stuff about the locket? Nope.'

'So he hasn't let it get to him?' her mom double-checked.

'No, Mom, really. He was joking and fooling around like always.'

'Yee-hah!' he'd cried as, drenched to the skin and hatless, he'd roped the runaway and leaned all his weight back on his heels to prevent the calf taking off with him in tow. 'Look at that son of a gun bite the dust! Man, you ain't goin' nowhere. Except along the shute to meet the shoer, to get a nice new brand mark on that pretty little butt!'

'You mean, he doesn't care what guys are saying about him?' Matt obviously found it strange that Troy could ignore the rising tide of rumour surrounding Linda Rankin and the theft of the locket, until Kirstie came up with the simple answer.

'It's not that Troy doesn't care,' she pointed out. 'It's that he's totally full of himself and has a skin thick as buffalo hide. The fact is, Matt, he doesn't even notice!'

'Just one more phone call,' Sandy promised Kirstie, who was standing by the door anxious to set off for school.

Hadley stood beside her, hat in hand, offering information whenever it was asked.

'I already called two ranch owners out in Montana to check Troy's work record,' Kirstie's mom explained. 'So far, no problem. There was Ken Morehouse on the N Bar; he hired Troy a couple of years back for the fall round-up. Didn't have a bad word to say about him. And he recalls Silver Spur too. He says he was the best working horse he ever came across.'

Kirstie nodded enthusiastically. She liked the sound of this Ken Morehouse guy.

'Then Hadley told me to call Mary Lee Stewart out at the Double E. She's one of the toughest bosses around. It turns out she never hired Troy herself, but she heard through a friend that he was the main man. She tells me she tried to hire him this spring, but it turned out he was off the map. When I said I'd hired him down in Colorado to lead trail-rides, she swore it was a waste of real talent.'

'But she didn't mention the problem with Red Owen?' Kirstie asked.

'Nope. Only that she's looking forward to seeing Troy and Silver Spur compete in Dallas next month. I figure she plans to headhunt him for the Double E!'

'That's great.' Kirstie felt that this settled things. 'So why make another phone call?'

'Hadley reckons we should go straight to the horse's mouth, in other words, call the Three Rs direct.'

Kirstie frowned and watched her mom punch in the numbers. Personally she found this way over-the-top and felt irritated with the old wrangler for pushing things. Weren't two good reports enough to clear a guy's name?

Hadley waited nearby. His lean, lined face gave no sign of any emotion. Things would turn out whichever way they would, without him bothering his head.

'Yeah, OK, I hear you. Mr Owen isn't home.' Sandy spoke loudly down an obviously bad line. 'I'm talking to his head wrangler, Jerome Shapiro, is that correct? . . . Yeah, listen, I need to ask your advice on an employee here named Troy Hendren.'

Kirstie watched her mom's expression as the

57

response came through, noting the crease form between her eyes. Apparently, the answer was long, loud and totally clear.

She already knew what Shapiro had said before Sandy put down the receiver.

'He confirmed the rifle story,' she sighed. 'Gave me a couple more details, like the reason they didn't go ahead and prosecute Troy was because he discharged himself from the hospital before they had time to bring in the sheriff to arrest him. There's still a county warrant out for him.'

'Bad news,' Hadley grunted, turning the rim of his hat slowly between his blunt, gnarled fingers.

'What Shapiro told me, word for word before he hung up was, "Troy Hendren and his horse may be good at what they do, but boy, doesn't the guy let you know it. And who wants a mouthy, flashy cowboy you can't trust? Not me, that's for sure. And neither does any sane ranch owner this side of the Rocky Mountains!" '

'Yes ma'am!' Hadley agreed. Still awkwardly fingering his hat, he let slip the reason why he'd thought it a good idea all along to check up on the newcomer's credentials. 'Like I said, he don't know when to keep his mouth shut, and that ain't never a good sign.'

'But you can't condemn a guy just for talking too much!' Kirstie protested. Though the facts against Troy seemed to be piling up, she still felt unwilling to believe the worst.

'Yeah, and you can't trust him just for riding a horse real good,' Hadley countered. 'I seen plenty of good cowboys in my time who I wouldn't trust further than I could throw 'em. Besides, there's somethin' I ain't told you yet.'

'What is it?' Sandy demanded.

Hadley sniffed and stared down at his boots, reluctant to play the informer, but feeling duty bound. 'You recall that Troy and the kid with the blond hair . . .'

'Joe Stefan,' Kirstie reminded him.

'Yeah, him. Well they brought the fifteen steers in from Eden Lake early yesterday afternoon. Ben and you were still out with your groups looking for more cattle.'

'That's right,' Sandy said impatiently. 'So?'

'So I was takin' a rest in my cabin and I seen Troy unsaddle his paint and take him and Jitterbug out to the meadow like you'd expect. But then what happened next struck me as strange. Instead of going right into the bunkhouse, to take a shower and pretty himself up for the cook-out, he came climbing the path alongside my cabin, kinda lookin' around but not noticin' I was there.'

'And he carried on up to Hummingbird at the back of you, is that what you're saying?' Sandy demanded.

Hadley nodded, his voice hardly more than a murmur. 'Yes ma'am, you got it. I'm saying that's exactly what he did.'

5

'So, girls, you wanna ride with me today?' Troy called across the corral to Tessa and Hayley Eastmann.

With a heavy heart Kirstie stepped out of the house into the yard, aware that this was building up to what looked like a bad day for their new wrangler. Already late for school, she'd left her mom and Matt working out what to do after Hadley's latest revelation.

'You gotta confront the guy,' Matt had insisted. 'We can't afford to let this slip by.'

But Sandy had still shown signs of wanting to

delay. 'Let me talk to Brad,' she'd pleaded. 'I want his input before I take action.'

Kirstie had left them to it and wandered outside.

'Hey, Tessa; d'you and your sister want to come lookin' for cows with the professionals?' Troy repeated, riding up close to where the two girls waited on Snowflake and Squeaky.

The little, dark-haired girl gave an embarrassed shrug and turned to her older sister.

'Mom said we had to stick with Sandy's group,' Hayley explained quietly.

'She did, huh?' Troy seemed taken aback. 'I thought you told me that my group had the most fun roundin' up those steers. And I'm headin' up to Dorfmann Lake. We'll find plenty of cows up in that territory.'

'Yeah, well . . .' It was Hayley's turn to blush and shrug, reining Squeaky to one side and sidling away from Troy.

'Hey Troy, does that mean I get to ride with you again today?' Joe Stefan led Jitterbug across the corral to put in a special request.

But this time the snub was so in-your-face that even Troy couldn't miss it.

'Joe!' A loud voice called him back. It was his

father, Dave Stefan, openly forbidding his son to go talk with the wrangler.

'Give me a break, Dad!' Joe protested.

'Joe, I'm fixing for us to stick around the ranch today, do some chores, maybe go fishing later.' Dave Stefan was dead set on spoiling the boy's day and on making it plain to everyone within earshot that he didn't want Joe spending any time in Troy's company.

Downcast, Joe turned Jitterbug towards the row-stalls, giving in to the pressure and resigning himself to a boring day without riding.

'Huh.' Left stranded by the fence, Troy caught sight of Kirstie waiting for her ride into town. 'What did I do?'

His handsome face had lost its jaunty expression and looked genuinely upset.

'Nothing. Forget it,' Kirstie said quickly, aware that Alicia Rankin and her mother were walking down from their cabin to begin the day's ride. Once they arrived on the scene, the atmosphere would grow even worse than it was already.

'Is it somethin' I said?' Troy glanced around the corral to see that every single guest had averted their gaze and was suddenly absorbed in tightening an important buckle or straightening the blanket beneath their horse's saddle.

'Just let it drop,' Kirstie insisted. She picked up the poisonous looks coming from both of the Rankins as they passed close by.

'Jeez, some guys are so thick-skinned you wouldn't believe it!' Linda said loud enough for Troy to hear.

Then she and Alicia called to Ben on the far side of the corral, demanding to know what had been done about extra security for their cabin.

'I can't sleep for thinkin' that some sneak thief is gonna break in in the middle of the night!' she complained, with an obvious look back in Troy's direction. 'Literally, I didn't get a wink last night. The same with Alicia, we were both scared to death!'

'Jeez!' Troy shook his head and stared after the mother and daughter. 'Give me strength!'

You still don't get it! Kirstie thought. And it seemed cruel to leave the poor guy in the dark. Besides, the way everyone was acting, it couldn't be long before the light dawned even inside Troy's dim head.

So, climbing on to the bottom rail of the fence and fondling Silver Spur's white muzzle as she talked, she did him the favour of breaking the bad news.

'They think it's you!' she explained through gritted teeth. 'Linda Rankin put out certain feelers, picked up a couple of pieces of information from a cousin in Billings and started putting two and two together . . .'

Kirstie watched Troy's face crease as he slowly absorbed what she was telling him. He frowned deeply and his grey eyes narrowed to slits. Tense muscles jumped all along the line of his bottom jaw.

Silver Spur too picked up the seriousness of the situation, raising his head and pricking his ears as if on the lookout for sudden danger.

'So I guess I'm the villain again,' Troy muttered in a bitter tone.

'I didn't say that!' Kirstie hissed back. 'I'm only saying that's the rumour Linda Rankin's spreading . . .'

Across the corral, she could see Alicia Rankin staring their way with a strange, gloating smile on her face. Evidently she realised even from that distance what was going on between Troy and Kirstie.

'Yeah, well . . .' Angrily Troy turned Silver Spur towards the gate. 'Tell the boss I'm headin' out solo, to Dorfmann to look for cattle.'

'Troy!' Kirstie didn't want him to simply ride away. She wanted to tell him that not everyone believed the woman's accusation.

But he kept on riding. 'Roundin' up steers is what I'm paid for,' he insisted, cutting a path through horses and guests, who quickly stood to one side. 'And until Sandy Scott tells me different, that's what me and my horse plan to do!'

'Bad day?' Kirstie's best friend, Lisa Goodman, caught up with her during recess. 'Or is that scowl you're wearing part of a new, brooding image designed to keep the world at arm's length?'

'Sorry.' Making room for Lisa on the bench below the library window, Kirstie managed a faint smile.

'Trouble back at the ranch?' Lisa guessed, easing her trousers up as far as her knees so that her legs could get some time in the sun. She gazed idly at kids crossing the school campus carrying books and talking into cell phones.

'Yeah,' Kirstie sighed. All morning, the problem of Troy Hendren had been on her mind.

'So tell me.'

'No, you wouldn't be interested. Staff problems, y'know.'

Lisa studied Kirstie hard from beneath her fringe of wavy auburn hair. 'Since when was I bored with anything that happens at Half-Moon Ranch? C'mon, try me!'

So Kirstie brought Lisa up to speed with the problem, gathering pace as she talked. 'The problem is, it does look bad for Troy,' she admitted. 'And Mom realises that maybe she should have checked him out more thoroughly before she offered him the job. Only, with Charlie leaving so suddenly, what choice did she have? And Troy did come with Brad's recommendation . . .'

'Whoa!' Lisa put up both hands to slow her down. 'Here's the bottom line: d'*you* think Troy stole the locket?'

Asked point-blank, Kirstie found she didn't even hesitate. 'No way!'

'Why not?'

'Because . . . call it gut feeling. I don't know. Troy may be flashy, but he's straight as they come. Besides, he's good to his horse!'

'Oh well then!' Lisa laughed. 'Yeah, yeah, don't get mad. I see what you mean. If a guy treats his horse nice, it kinda spills over to his dealings with people.'

'Yeah!' That was it exactly. 'Anyhow, there's a dozen other suspects if you really think it through.'

'So, who?' Lisa's responses were quick and sharp. 'C'mon, give me the list.'

This time Kirstie's answer came more slowly.

'Well, for a start, it could be a complete outsider – an intruder.'

'You're kidding! The ranch is way off the beaten track, remember. Anyone driving down that Shelf-Road is sure to be spotted before he even sets foot on the place!' Lisa crossed off Kirstie's first anonymous suspect without a second thought. 'Next!'

'OK, well it could be a kid called Joe Stefan. He was back early with Troy at the time this theft is alleged to have taken place. So he'd be free to wander into the cabins and poke through guests'

belongings for anything worth stealing.'

'How old is Joe?' Lisa asked.

'Ten or eleven.'

Lisa gave Kirstie one of her long, you-must-be-kidding-me stares.

'OK, maybe not.' Once more Kirstie backed down. 'So what if Linda Rankin just lost the locket? She's the type who could get all worked up into thinking it had been stolen.'

'Better.' Lisa took this theory on board. 'But if it had been just lost, wouldn't it have turned up by now?'

Slowly Kirstie nodded. 'I guess. And anyway, I actually went into Hummingbird to help the Rankins search. I'm pretty convinced that they know where every last hairpin and ten-cent biro is kept. OK, here's another possibility. Linda Rankin has this daughter, Alicia. A moody type. Well, maybe you would come across that way if your dad had just died last fall—'

'Jeez, poor kid,' Lisa cut in. 'You didn't tell me that earlier.'

'I didn't figure it was important until now.'

Lisa picked up her point. 'You're thinking the family tragedy maybe sent the daughter a little weird?'

'Yeah. She doesn't talk to the other kids. She looks pretty unhappy most of the time, comes across as a nasty type who enjoys other people getting into trouble.'

'Stop! Already I don't like her!' Lisa exclaimed. 'And I haven't even met the girl! And I think you could have something. You say she seems glad that Troy, for instance, is having a hard time?'

Recalling the sly, sideways look and the covert smile on Alicia's face earlier that morning when she came down to the corral, Kirstie nodded. 'I'm wondering, could she have hidden the locket and set the whole thing up for someone else to get the blame? Twisted, yeah. But possible, huh?'

'Yeah, but why would she make Troy the target?' Lisa wondered, rolling down her trousers and gathering her books from the bench. They'd just heard the end of recess bell ring loud and clear.

'Maybe she didn't. Maybe that's just how it turned out.' The deeper Kirstie got into this, the more possible it seemed to become. 'On the other hand, maybe she was the one who sowed the seed in her mom's mind by reminding her that Troy had worked at Red Owen's place where there'd been all that trouble . . .'

'You lost me there,' Lisa confessed, beginning the

walk back towards their classroom.

'Yeah, that bit's complicated. But it makes sense to me,' Kirstie insisted. They entered the cool building, squinting until their eyes adjusted to the shadows. 'And hey, I just remembered a definite reason for Alicia to get this hate thing against Troy!'

Lisa-the-would-be-psychiatry-major nodded and said 'hmm', as if the two of them were scientifically uncovering the layers of Alicia Rankin's personality.

'Troy teased Alicia during her saddle-fitting when they first arrived at the ranch. And he did it again at the cook-out. I tell you, at that moment, if looks could have killed, he'd have been dead!'

It was a small thing; hardly noticeable. But then small things tipped mixed-up people over the edge. Lisa said yeah, it was out of proportion but possible, maybe . . .

When you really thought it through – and Kirstie did, this way and that for the whole afternoon – this entire locket thing could be poor Alicia Rankin's twisted way of getting her revenge!

'Troy, can you give me a couple of seconds of your time?' Polite and businesslike as ever, Ben called across the arena to the wrangler who was about to begin an early evening training session with Silver Spur.

Kirstie had arrived home from school determined to push her new theory a little further by explaining it to her mom. But Sandy had driven over to Brad's place near San Luis to confer with him over the problem that had developed with Troy. She wouldn't be back until after supper, Matt had told her, adding that he didn't see what else there was to talk about, now that they'd heard the detailed reasons from Jerome Shapiro behind Troy's departure from the Three Rs.

So Kirstie had gone out to hang around the corral and watch Troy work with his horse. She'd already taken in the fact that, instead of the enthusiastic crowd of previous occasions, today none of the other guests had chosen to come and spectate. And now Ben had serious business to discuss with Troy. *Surely not!* Kirstie thought. Then a moment later: *No, of course.* It would be Sandy who must broach the subject of Troy having to leave. She heaved a sigh of relief and realised that Ben's conversation was about the round-up.

'We're under pressure,' he confided in Troy, who had ridden across to speak with his boss. 'You brought sixteen cows down from Dorfmann and my group brought in a total of twenty. Twenty plus sixteen plus seventy-eight makes . . .'

'One hundred and fourteen,' Troy calculated quickly. 'Leaving eighty-six still out there.'

'And only three days to find them,' Ben pointed out.

'Problem is, those steers could be scattered far and wide. And they sure don't want to be caught and brought down from those lush green pastures.' Troy gave the benefit of his experience with a closed, distracted air. Kirstie could tell that his mind wasn't fully on what Ben went on to say.

'I figure we need to ride out north towards Aspen Park,' Ben decided. 'There's good winter pasture up there and plenty of draws with water and willow thickets for cows to lose themselves in. How about we split the dude riders into two tomorrow. You take half and I take half, and we both work our way up to Aspen Park?'

'Yeah, if I still have a job tomorrow,' Troy muttered. 'If you really wanna know, I feel like the guy on Death Row waiting for them to flick that switch!'

Ben shot him a look from under the brim of his stetson. 'That ain't none of my business. Like you, I

73

just do my work. And my job is to give you the orders about what we need to do tomorrow, which is to bring in as many of those eighty-six cows as we can find.' Plain and simple.

Kirstie smiled. Trust Ben to cut through the garbage. And she could see that his attitude had given Troy a small boost.

'Gotcha,' he said, nodding and turning Silver Spur back into the centre of the arena. 'C'mon, boy, we ain't got no time to waste yakking. We got a ropin' contest to win in Dallas, remember!'

Kirstie too felt the tension lift as she sat on the fence in the low sunlight to watch the paint horse go through his paces.

Silver Spur used the arena to hone his roping and cutting manoeuvres, his muscles bunched with the hard exercise of loping, turning and executing lead-changes in quick succession. Soon his withers were sweating in the heat, and his nostrils noisily sucked in air. Every move was precise and balanced as he went willingly into one exercise after another.

Brilliant! Kirstie breathed. She loved the scene: horse and rider a perfect team, raising dust against the backdrop of the red barn roof and beyond that, above the pine-covered foothills, the low sun setting slowly on to the jagged horizon.

Into her mind a saying floated. It had been the favourite of her grandpa when he ran Half-Moon Ranch as a real working cattle spread. Ranching had been his whole life and he'd often reminded his grand-daughter of the importance of treating the horse who worked with you exactly right.

'The right feed, the right amount of work – not too much, not too little or he'll turn lazy and ornery. And y'know, there's something about the outside of a horse that's good for the inside of a man!'

Maybe Kirstie hadn't understood that at the time. She must have been eight or nine years old when he'd passed the remark, before she and her mom and Matt had taken over the ranch. But it had stayed with her all these years, and she sure saw what her grandpa had meant now as she sat in the setting sun and watched Silver Spur. 'Something about the outside of a horse . . .' The flowing motion of the powerful, loping stride, the beautiful head, the streaming mane and tail. It sure made you feel good inside just to sit and watch.

Until the peace was broken by the New York State guest who was staying in one of the older cabins beyond the barn. John Pitts came running alongside the corral, yelling for Ben or Matt or 'any so-and-so who had some position of authority around this darned place.'

Kirstie clocked the angry tone. *What now?* she wondered. Pitts wasn't the type to yell and scream over nothing.

Then Matt came out of the house, and the guest made a bee-line for him. 'OK,' he yelled, holding both hands high and spreading them wide. 'We knew it would happen to some other poor sucker sooner or later, and I guess I'm the one!'

'Hold it,' Matt protested. 'You gotta slow down and give it to me straight.'

Pitts stopped waving his arms around and held his hands out in a steadying gesture. 'OK, get this,' he began.

As he took a deep breath, Troy brought Silver Spur around the arena and reined him to a halt behind Kirstie. He took in every word John Pitts said.

'A whole lot of stuff has gone missing from my cabin,' he told Matt, keeping calm but at the same time demanding fast action. 'I lost a watch, a video-camera and seven hundred dollars in cash. And right now I need to know what you're gonna do about it!'

6

'But why seven hundred dollars?' was Sandy's question when she arrived back at the ranch to be greeted by the latest piece of bad news. She'd invited John Pitts and Linda Rankin into the house to discuss what they wanted to do next. 'Why not take the rest of the money you say you had stashed away in the closet?'

The New York investment adviser shrugged and shook his head. 'Who knows what's going on in a guy's head when he breaks into a place? All I'm saying is, he left three hundred lying in the drawer and took seven. Plus of course the video camera, worth in excess of a thousand dollars, and a Swiss wristwatch which was a gift from my ex-wife. And I'll say this about Connie: she may have made my life a misery when I was married to her, but she never bought anything cheap. Especially if it was my dough she was spending.'

Kirstie saw her mom give way to a wan smile.

'So you'd like me to talk to Troy?' Sandy asked.

Linda Rankin and John Pitts were together on this one. 'We sure do,' Linda insisted. 'And we want to be here when you do.'

'Are you certain you want to do this?' Kirstie's mom looked uneasy about a head-on confrontation. 'You know we don't have a scrap of hard evidence against Troy. And accusing a guy of theft, at the same time as putting his job in jeopardy, is a pretty serious move.'

Kirstie found herself nodding at this, though she wasn't part of the conversation. It seemed clear to her that her mom's talk with Brad earlier that afternoon had come up with the same information as before – that Troy was a straight down the line, regular guy who would never get involved in anything underhand. Which was why Sandy was still reluctant to act.

But John Pitts was a tougher guy to deal with

than fussy, semi-neurotic Linda Rankin. He was a clean-shaven, clear-thinking businessman with rimless glasses and a cut-and-dried manner. And his expensive vacation had been blemished by a temporary blip that needed to be handled efficiently. In other words, he wanted action.

'Listen,' he told Sandy. 'First, there was the stolen locket. You held back on that until you'd checked out a few facts. Now, we have this second incident, which might not have occurred if you'd made your move right away.'

Sandy frowned. She couldn't argue against this.

'So I stand to lose property worth a total of in excess of three thousand dollars. Tomorrow, some guy down the track in some other cabin could lose a whole lot more . . .'

'Yeah, sure,' Kirstie's mom sighed. 'OK, let me go bring Troy in and we'll try to settle this thing.'

Before she could turn and reach the door, Kirstie had stepped across her path. 'I'll go find him,' she murmured, recalling his grim image of the man on Death Row.

She found Troy unsaddling Silver Spur in a row-stall after his training work in the arena. The horse blew noisily after his hard work, standing head down in the old sleepy position that misled you into thinking he was some old, bored kiddie horse without an ounce of pep left in him.

As Kirstie approached, Troy looked up over his horse's back and read the dark expression on her face. 'Don't tell me,' he muttered, stepping out of the stall, his face hidden under the shadow of his hat. 'The boss wants to see me.'

She nodded and walked back across the corral with him, then over the yard, half-running to match his long stride, and up under the porch into the house, where they walked into a stiff, awkward silence.

Troy took in John Pitts's and Linda Rankin's presence. Then he turned to look directly at Sandy. 'Boss, if you wanna fire me, go ahead and do it,' he said quietly.

'Don't you want a chance to defend yourself?' Sandy asked.

'How can I, when I don't even know what I'm supposed to have done?' Troy's manner was resigned, his eyes focused on the striped mat that covered the polished wooden floor.

'C'mon, don't give me that!' John Pitts cut in. 'There have been two thefts in two days around here, and the finger is pointing directly at you, buddy!'

Drawing a deep breath, Troy hung his head lower still. 'Like I said, go ahead and fire me,' he invited Sandy. 'Get it over with.'

'But are you saying you didn't have anything to do with either of these – incidents?' Sandy prised a denial out of him, willing him to stand up for himself.

'What's it matter what I say?'

'Right!' Linda Rankin challenged with a mean look. 'A guy with a warrant out for his arrest in Billings County doesn't have much of a leg to stand on when it comes to wanting people to believe his side of a story!'

Kirstie saw Troy flinch and clench his jaw tight shut.

'But Troy, are you telling us you're innocent?' Sandy insisted.

Good job! Kirstie breathed. Trust her mom to give a guy every chance!

Troy nodded. 'Yes, ma'am.'

Satisfied, Sandy turned to John Pitts and Linda Rankin. 'Here's what I plan to do. First thing tomorrow I call the sheriff.'

'Not before time!' Linda said bitterly 'We need the law to deal with this pronto.'

'Next, you fire Hendren,' John predicted.

But Sandy shook her head. 'No. And before you come on heavy, let me say that I'm a believer in regarding a man as innocent until proven guilty. With the stress on "proven"!' She outstared her two angry guests and had the rest of her say. 'So, we bring in Sheriff Francini. He investigates the whole deal. Meanwhile, if Troy agrees to stick it out, I say he carries out his duties as per usual!'

'You will stay, won't you?' After the head to head, Kirstie walked back with Troy to the row-stalls. 'You won't just take off?'

The sun was gone behind Eagle's Peak; the short dusk cloaked the barn in shadows.

'What's to stick around for?' Troy shrugged. He untied the slip-knot on Silver Spur's lead-rope and trudged him off towards Red Fox Meadow. 'My job here is to lead guys on trail-rides and bring in cattle with 'em. And look what happened: nobody wants to ride with me. They all think I got two heads.'

'No they don't!' Kirstie insisted.

'So who doesn't?'

'Joe Stefan doesn't . . . I don't!' Kirstie had to admit that Troy's supporters were few and far between. 'Y'know, part of your problem is that you come across as so – well, so full of yourself!'

Surprised by what she'd just come out with, she held her breath and waited for Troy's reaction.

'So that makes me an out-and-out thief, does it?' he muttered, allowing Kirstie to cross the footbridge over Five Mile Creek ahead of him and Silver Spur.

'No, of course not! But maybe some people find it hard to take.'

'You mean I'm an obnoxious jerk and a waste of space!' Troy had the grace to grin.

'Yeah, totally,' she joked back, running ahead to open the meadow gate. Across the field, the horses had bunched together in the dim light, mere silhouettes against the white rails of the long fence.

'Gee thanks for putting me straight on that.' Troy unbuckled Silver Spur's headcollar and let him loose in the meadow. For a few seconds the paint hung around by the gate, nudging Troy's shoulder in a friendly way. 'Beat it!' Troy insisted, giving the horse's rump a light tap.

So Silver Spur set off at a trot, kicking up divots of dry earth, stretching into a lope and then a full gallop as he went to join the others.

'Why don't you explain a couple of things to me?' Kirstie invited, feeling closer to Troy now that she'd stepped over the usual polite boundaries. *I mean, I just told the guy he was a flashy know-all!* she reminded herself. *And he didn't bite my head off of my shoulders!*

'Like what?' Standing in the entrance to the long, flat meadow, Troy stared after Silver Spur.

'Like, what were you doing up by Hummingbird at the time when Linda Rankin's locket was stolen?' *Big question, big risk.* Kirstie held her breath.

'Who told you that?' Troy asked sharply.

'Hadley saw you pass by his cabin.'

'Yeah, OK.' Troy paused.

Was he using the delay to invent an excuse, she wondered.

'I was there,' he admitted. 'If I recall correctly, I'd untacked Jitterbug and Silver Spur then watered them and brought them out here. And when I was putting away the saddles, I came across Joe's baseball cap, tucked away inside his saddle-bag. I thought maybe the kid would need it for the cook-out, so yeah, I took the track up past Brown Bear and Hummingbird, and I went right on to Elkhorn, which is the Stefans' cabin, and left the cap right there on the porch-swing because there was no one home.'

Kirstie nodded eagerly. 'So we could check that out?'

'Sure.'

'OK, good.' Encouraged, Kirstie drew up her

courage to ask Troy the even bigger question. 'So what about the warrant for your arrest over in Billings?'

'Yeah, Linda Rankin,' Troy murmured. 'She's so on-the-ball she should set up a private detective agency!'

'Don't dodge the issue!' The stars beginning to twinkle in the sky, the rising crescent moon, somehow made Kirstie feel bolder. 'Did you steal an antique rifle, or didn't you?'

'You want the whole thing, or edited highlights?'

'The whole thing!'

'OK. No, I didn't steal it.'

'Is that it?' she protested. 'C'mon, Troy; if you want me to believe your version, you have to give me it first!'

'It's a mess,' he sighed. 'And it means I have to bad-mouth a guy I once respected.'

'Whose name is Red Owen?' she prompted.

'Yeah. He's highly regarded back home in Montana. He sits on big rodeo committees, does some good charity work.'

'But?'

'The guy don't treat horses right,' Troy mumbled. 'More especially, I found him not treating *my* horse properly. Now, normally I can stand a whole lot of garbage from a man who pays my salary, but when I come across him taking the flat side of a spade to Silver Spur's head, I pretty soon reach the end of my tether.'

Kirstie gasped. 'Red Owen was beating up Silver Spur?'

He nodded. 'Big-time. The horse was rearing up and straining to break free from his rope. Owen had raised the spade over his shoulder, ready to whack it across Silver's skull.'

As he stumbled over the story, Kirstie picked out the black-and-white patched shape of Troy's horse gallop the length and breadth of the meadow, then turn and head back towards them. It was as if in some supersensitive way he'd tuned in to Troy's pain at the retelling of events.

'So what did you do?' she whispered.

'I threw myself at the guy and grabbed the spade. He hung on tight and caught me off-balance, kept the tool in his hand as a weapon and came at me while I lay in the dirt. He smashed the blade down across my jaw and that's all I recall.'

'And did you ever find out why he'd planned to beat Silver Spur?'

'My guess is, he'd been drinking. That was the word around the ranch, that he had a drink problem and easily lost control. I figure Silver Spur had objected to the rough way Owen tied him up and let him know it. Then the guy just lost it, picked up the spade and started to hit out.'

By this time, the paint had returned to where they stood, slowed his pace and come sidling up against Troy's shoulder. Half closing his eyes, he came across with his dopey look, which Kirstie now began to recognise as affection. Half-closed eyes meaning, *Give me some lovin'*!

'So you wake up in hospital to find out that Owen's been spreading rumours and lies – he's blaming you for the fight and people are believing him?'

'Yeah, and worse,' Troy went on, absently stroking his horse's neck. 'To cover up the real reason, he ups and takes his rifle from its showplace over the fire, he takes it over to the bunkhouse and stashes it under my bunk. Then he sends his head wrangler, Jerome Shapiro, with a team of men out looking for it, maybe dropping a heavy hint that my bunk is the place to search. And what d'you know, they find it wrapped in a blanket right where Owen put it. They call in the sheriff, who heads right on over to the hospital to arrest me.'

'But you leave before he gets there?' Kirstie shook

her head. 'Not a smart move in my opinion!'

'You figure I should've waited to be framed and slung in jail?' Troy hooked his arm over the horse's neck and breathed a few soothing words into his ear. 'Then what would've happened to this poor guy, huh? You reckon Owen would've wanted him on the Triple R reminding him what really happened once I was off the scene? No way. Knowing him, he'd have shipped Silver off for dogmeat before the week was up.'

Once more, Kirstie found herself drawing a sharp breath. 'Gotcha. So you hightailed it back to the ranch with a severe jaw ache to sneak in and pick up Silver Spur. Then, knowing that Mr Rodeo-Ranch-Boss would blacken your name up and down the county, you put a county border between you and trouble?'

Troy nodded. 'We spent the winter bumming around a few places in north western Colorado: Boulder, Aspen, a few of the ski resorts. I got menial jobs, took care of Silver Spur, lived in a beat-up trailer. Come early spring, I got back into competition, trained for New Jersey, and that's where I met up again with my old buddy, Brad Martin, who put me in touch with your mom . . . And the rest, as they say, is history.'

7

'So when you meet Larry Francini, you tell it like it was,' Kirstie insisted. She felt certain that anyone who listened to Troy's story with an open mind would be bound to believe him.

It was early Thursday – an occasional holiday from school for her due to teacher training, and the day when they expected the San Luis sheriff to call.

Troy took Kirstie's earnest instructions in good spirit. 'Cool it, OK?' he answered as they scooped poop in the corral. The dung went into giant bins which were then tractored off for burning. 'Did your mom say exactly when the sheriff's gonna show up?'

'In the afternoon. He has to appear as a witness in court first. Depending on how long they need him, he should be out here around two.'

'And you figure he'll poke around askin' questions before he makes his move?' Troy needed to hear that Francini was a reasonable type, who only acted on facts and not hearsay.

'Sure, Larry's OK,' she reassured him. 'Anyhow, you can clear your mind while you ride out for cows this morning. And since I plan on coming along with you, you can talk to me about it any time you want.'

Finishing their task, they propped their broad spades against the side of the tack-room, then picked up a stack of headcollars and walked out together to bring horses in from the meadow.

'For starters, Larry's gonna be asking Linda and Alicia to run through the exact sequence of events around the time when Linda realised the locket was gone.' Talking about the forthcoming investigation made Kirstie feel more confident. 'I don't know why – I still have the feeling that things aren't right there . . .'

'Hey, hold it!' Troy told her that he appreciated what she was saying, but that putting a brake on the guesswork until the sheriff had asked the right questions might be a good idea.

'It's not guesswork!' Kirstie protested. 'If you watch Alicia close up, the way I have, you'd be saying the same as me, that there's something weird—'

'Whoa! What are you sayin' here – that the kid stole her own mother's jewellery, and that set her off on a major crime-spree?' Troy laid it on the line so that Kirstie would have to acknowledge the weakness of her theory.

'Maybe!' she insisted. 'I talked with my friend Lisa about it. We both think a thing like your father dying can send you off the rails.'

'Yeah well, you and your friend Lisa should take it easy with the accusations. These things spread like wildfire once they take hold,' Troy warned her, approaching Jitterbug and sliding the collar round his head. 'And I should know,' he added.

'But think about it.' The stubborn part of Kirstie's personality made her dig in her heels. She caught Lucky and then Squeaky, still pushing the same point. 'Isn't there something you've noticed about Alicia Rankin that doesn't quite add up?'

Troy shrugged. 'She's not exactly the party-party-party type, I guess. In fact, I don't think I ever heard her speak.' He stopped, deep in thought for a second. 'Come to think of it, not even when I figure she should.'

'Like when?' Kirstie asked quickly, seeing that Troy had been struck by a sudden realisation.

'Like the time Hadley was putting me in the frame for the theft from Hummingbird. Would Alicia have heard about that?'

Kirstie thought then nodded. 'Sure. Linda Rankin would go through it a dozen times once she got to know that Hadley saw you walk up towards the cabins. Alicia would be sick of hearing about it. Why do you ask?'

'Because that's a time when I reckon the girl would've spoken out and told her mom that she was there too and she saw exactly what I did.'

Stopping in her tracks, Kirstie frowned. 'Say that again. Alicia Rankin saw you walk past her cabin to Elkhorn and leave Joe's cap in the porch? How come?'

'She didn't ride that afternoon. Didn't anyone pick up on that?'

Kirstie felt her heartbeat quicken with fresh suspicion as she shook her head. The fact that Alicia had been inside the cabin most of the afternoon certainly cut down the opportunities for a sneak thief to creep in. And how weird was it that neither Linda nor the girl had thought to mention it. Triumphantly storing up the new piece of information, she and Troy headed back with half a dozen horses to the corral.

Half an hour later, after all the horses had been brought in and Kirstie was busy helping Ben and Troy to tack and saddle them, Sandy came out to organise the day with the head wrangler.

'I'd like you two guys to head out to Aspen Park together,' she decided, 'taking half the guests with you. Come midday, Troy, I'd like you to ride back to the ranch to speak with Sheriff Francini.'

'Yes ma'am,' he agreed, disguising any uneasiness he might feel.

'Matt and I will take the other half north too, since my guess is that's where most of the cattle are hiding out.'

'What about me?' Kirstie chipped in. 'Can I ride with Troy?'

Sandy shook her head. 'Sorry, honey. I'd like you to stay here and help Ray Pickett brand the last few calves as we bring them in.'

'Oh gee . . . !' She began a protest then saw from the firm look on her mom's face that there was no point arguing. And anyhow, this way she'd definitely be around when the sheriff arrived.

'OK, good.' Her mom seemed satisfied. 'You can leave Lucky saddled up in the corral, just in case. But if you're hoping to get a ride out on your day off school, all I can say is don't hold your breath.'

'Actually, Lucky just lost a shoe,' Kirstie told the blacksmith after they'd been hanging around the barn area for half an hour.

Ray Pickett had arrived soon after the round-up groups had headed out, racing his by-now familiar red and silver pick-up down the drive in his usual macho style.

At first he'd shown some irritation at the fact that there was nothing for him to do right away. 'I could've called in a couple of other places,' he'd complained. 'Earned myself some extra dough before I came out here if I'd known there were no calves to brand. And man, do I need the money!'

'Mom had a lot on her mind; I guess she forgot to firm up a time with you' Kirstie explained. Then she realised that in fact Ray was happy enough to lounge against the barn door, chewing tobacco and reading the sport pages of his newspaper. Then when she recalled that her palomino had thrown a shoe by accidentally kicking his hoof against the row-stall, she seized the chance to get it fixed.

'My bag of tools is still in the pick-up,' Ray grunted. 'I didn't expect to do no shoein' today, just brandin'.'

'It's OK, I'll fetch them.' Trying not to mind his offhand reaction, she ran to the truck.

Blacksmiths' tools were bulky; they would most likely be in the back of the pick-up, not the cab. So she climbed over the tailboard and began to search around amongst a heap of ropes, plastic bags, an old hunting rifle and crumpled newspapers. She noted without paying much attention that many of the papers were opened at the racing pages, and that Ray had highlighted in lime-green the names of certain horses on which evidently he wanted to place money.

Ray's a gambling man, she thought casually. *But he's no good at picking winners, to judge by this wreck of a pick-up he drives around in.*

'Try the passenger seat!' the smith yelled across the yard at her.

So she climbed out of the messed-up back and swung open the cab door, reaching inside for the heavy bag containing hammer, pliers and a jumble of other tools that Ray would need.

As she heaved at the bag and lifted it down from the cab, she happened to see a sheet of clean white paper slip to the ground. Thinking that it might be important, she stooped to pick it up and put it back on the seat. As she did so, she caught sight of a number printed large at the top of the sheet.

What's this? Looking again at the handwritten note, she read more closely.

'IOU the sum of $700.' Signed 'Ray Pickett'. Dated 5th April. Kirstie took this in, then glanced at the business name printed across the bottom. 'Sunrise Loan Service, Main Street, Marlowe County.' And then at an official stamp printed crosswise across the sheet, which said in upper-case letters: 'PAID WITH THANKS, 19TH APRIL.'

'Did you find the tools?' Ray Pickett yelled irritably from the barn door.

'Yeah, sure!' Startled, Kirstie shoved the piece of paper back on to the seat and slammed the door.

Seven hundred dollars repaid yesterday by Ray Pickett to a loan company. Maybe a gambling debt, and most likely none of her business.

But seven hundred dollars. And just yesterday.

Suppose the Sunrise people were putting on the screws for repayment. Suppose Ray Pickett, an habitual gambler, was desperate to get out of trouble.

And there was a thousand dollars stashed in a drawer in a guest's cabin. And not a soul around to stop the shoer from walking in there, counting it out and putting it in his pocket!

It was half past ten when the upholder of law and order in San Luis County stepped out of his patrol car into the yard of Half-Moon Ranch.

Sheriff Larry Francini straightened up, adjusted the broad leather belt around his wide girth, then took a deep breath and stared up at the mountain range.

Breathing good air into his lungs, the sheriff took his time to register Kirstie's presence as she ran from the barn area to join him. Francini was the balding, ageing, take-it-easy type of sheriff whose laid back presence could often defuse a tense situation. But there was a sharp brain operating behind the easy manner, and years of experience to back it up.

'Hey!' Kirstie greeted him, ready to pounce with her news about Ray Pickett's $700 IOU. But first she needed to get through the formalities. 'How come you're not in court?'

97

'Key witness failed to show,' Francini said in a low, slow growl. 'Case got postponed. Figured I'd mosey on over here instead.'

'Mom wasn't expecting you 'til this afternoon. They're all out rounding up cows.'

'No problem,' the sheriff shrugged, then changed the subject. 'Do I smell fresh coffee brewin'?'

Kirstie smiled briefly. 'You sure do. Just follow me.'

But before she had time to lead him into the house and begin her big exposé of the secret gambling addict whom her mom had just hired to shoe their horses and brand their calves, they were intercepted by John Pitts and Linda Rankin.

'Sheriff!' John called, his voice demanding immediate attention. 'Jeez, we're happy you got here. We need to shape this thing up and enable you to make an arrest before the whole ranch falls apart!'

Kirstie saw Francini pause, one foot on the porch step. She noted the brief disappointment as he saw his cup of coffee get put on indefinite hold. Then he turned to do his duty.

'Linda and I figured we'd skip the round-up this morning,' John explained. 'Partly for security reasons. Y'know, this outfit doesn't have a single lock and key in the entire place. I mean, how sloppy is that!'

Pitts's fellow victim wasn't slow to come in with the criticisms either. Red-faced under the rising sun, her cheeks smeared with sunblock, she upped the pressure on the sheriff. 'Like, we could sue them for that, couldn't we?' she demanded in a strident voice.

'No, ma'am. I think you'll find that Sandy Scott's ranch brochure specifically informs you that the cabins don't have locks but that if guests wish to place valuable items in a safe she has in the office, then you're more'n welcome to do so.'

Yeah! Kirstie thought. *Thank you, Sheriff!*

Meanwhile, Francini settled his level gaze on the semi-hysterical woman, noting that a teenaged girl had snuck up behind. He obviously made the mother–daughter link but said nothing. Then he shifted his attention around the empty yard, observing the shoer's pick-up reflecting sunlight from its chrome fenders and Ray Pickett himself packing away his tools as Lucky stood newly shod in a stall nearby.

'Anyhow, it's good we stuck around.' John Pitts dragged them back to the main point. 'We get to sort this mess out earlier than we figured.'

'You have to make an arrest, Sheriff, and do us all a favour.' Linda's voice rose a pitch or two. 'Our vacations are turning into nightmares, believe me. And all because of some sneaky cowboy they've hired without first checking his history.'

'Ma'am,' Francini said politely, but without disguising an irritated frown. 'You wanna put a name to this cowboy?'

'I sure do. It's Troy Hendren who's behind these thefts. That's real plain, Sheriff. Ask anyone round here.'

Francini nodded then turned to John Pitts. 'Troy Hendren, huh?'

'Sure. He's the one with the warrant out against him. Plus, he had the opportunity.'

The sheriff nodded again then methodically passed on to Kirstie for her opinion. 'Troy Hendren?'

'No way!' Her answer practically exploded from her. It wasn't what John and Linda wanted to hear, but who cared? 'I could name a couple other people before I even began to consider Troy!'

'Such as?' Francini cocked his head to one side, waiting for an answer.

But this time, Kirstie managed to bite back her words. 'I can't say. I don't have enough evidence.'

Only the fact that Alicia had been around on the afternoon her mom's locket went walkabout. And only a debt for $700 repaid yesterday by a guy who was broke. Alicia and Pickett would call that coincidence and deny everything, for sure.

'Hmm.' The sheriff didn't push her. 'What d'you say you ride out and fetch Troy for me anyways?' he suggested instead.

Kirstie sighed. She knew that this part had to happen, but she found she couldn't fetch Troy back with as much confidence as she'd felt earlier. After all, she'd said, it would be an easy thing to clear his name; all he had to do was tell the sheriff the truth. No problem. But now, with John Pitts and Linda Rankin throwing around the accusations, she didn't feel so sure.

So she dragged her heels as she went to saddle Lucky. Poor Troy; things did seem pretty stacked against him. Kicking up the dust in the corral, Kirstie glanced up to catch the eye of Alicia Rankin still hovering in the background. *Yeah, you know more than you're tellin'!* she thought with a sudden, fierce clarity.

Alicia caught the look and quickly ducked her head. Then she raised it again with a defiant stare. 'Where's Yukon?' she demanded.

'She's in the row-stalls waiting for her rider,' Kirstie replied pointedly. 'The other guys all set out an hour ago. What kept you?'

'I guess I overslept,' Alicia sneered. 'That's no problem, I know my way up to Aspen Park by now.'

'Yeah, whatever.' Kirstie knew that by allowing a dude rider out on the trails solo she was breaking ranch Rule Number One. But frankly, she had other things on her mind and anyway Alicia Rankin wasn't in a mood to be stopped.

So she watched the stocky, pushy kid drag Yukon out of the stall, yanking at the brown-and-white paint's mouth and swinging roughly into the saddle.

Poor Yukon endured the treatment without reacting, even when Alicia dug her heels hard into her flanks.

'Hey, use a little lighter touch!' Larry Francini called out as horse and rider made for the corral gate.

Ignoring him, Alicia came up to the gate to find it firmly closed.

'Let me get it for you,' Kirstie offered, unable to disguise the sarcastic hostility in her voice.

Impatiently Alicia frowned down at her.

One dirty look too many. Holding on to the gate, Kirstie stared back. 'Are you gonna tell the sheriff where you were when that locket got stolen,' she hissed, 'or am I?'

She was recalling the answering look in Alicia Rankin's eye as she rode out to Aspen Park to fetch Troy.

It had been a wild look: dead scared, then angry. Then Alicia had closed her face down into mask-like immobility. 'Yeah!' she'd sneered. 'Like, you know everything, Miss Cowgirl-of-the-Year!'

Then she'd barged Yukon past Kirstie and headed off without listening to her mom's warnings about riding carefully and being sure not to lose her way.

Scared, then angry. Like, definitely guilty! Kirstie rode Lucky quickly across the brushwood stretch between two stands of ponderosa pines. She kept the sun to her right-hand side, heading north, cutting across country in her haste to reach Troy. Feeling the urgency in her body language, Lucky responded by breaking into a lope wherever he could.

OK, so Alicia was around Hummingbird for sure. So did she see the thief enter the cabin? Or was she the culprit? One or the other! Kirstie grew more certain.

So where do Ray and the IOU figure in all this? Maybe a guy with a whole heap of gambling debts would steal a valuable antique if the opportunity came his way. Maybe he'd paid off one debt and found the whole thing working out real neat. Why not try again? John Pitts was obviously a well-heeled guest. Try his cabin when no one was looking. Yeah; lottery-winner time! A camera, a watch worth who knows how much. Oh and while I'm here, maybe I'll take that seven hundred I owe to the Sunrise Loan people. That solves that little problem, du-dah!

But where was the Ray–Alicia link? This still didn't figure, Kirstie realised. *What connected them, so that maybe Alicia covered up for Ray when she caught him red-handed?* Nope, that bit of her theory still needed work.

Covering the ground fast, only taking it easy when she and Lucky came to a downhill stretch, Kirstie's thought process was interrupted by the sight of riders and cattle cresting a ridge to the north-west. Soon she made out Ben leading, and was able to count eight cows with seven calves. So she cut across to speak with the head wrangler.

'Good job!' she called as soon as she was within hearing. Amongst the riders in Ben's group were John Pitts's friend, Alvin Reed, another New York finance guy who was by now a natural at crying 'Yip! yip! C'mon, girls!' to a bunch of unwilling cattle.

Ben smiled back at her. 'We'll bring these in then ride out again after lunch.'

'So where's Troy? I need to take him back to speak with Sheriff Francini earlier than we figured,' she explained quietly.

Ben nodded. 'Troy split off to the north-east, looking for more cows. He took the Eastmann kids with him. I reckon they'll be in Aspen Park by this time.'

'Did Alicia Rankin find you yet?' Kirstie inquired.

'Nope. Why?'

'It's OK, forget it. Maybe she rode out to join mom's group.' Dismissing the problem, Kirstie gave the herd of bunched-up, barging cows a wide berth. Then she set off up a steep slope at a rapid trot. Aspen Park was two miles off maybe a ten to fifteen minute hard ride.

So they dodged tree trunks and ducked branches, made flying lead-changes round boulders and covered lots of dry, sage-scattered territory in the building heat.

Then, half a mile outside the winter pasture, Kirstie ran up against Hayley and Tessa Eastmann.

'How come?' she asked breathlessly, loping to meet the two girls beside a stack of felled timber. 'What happened? I heard you were with Troy?'

'We were,' Tessa gasped. 'But something happened, so he sent us back to the ranch, said to give the horses their heads because they knew the way. He said, tell the first guy we meet what we saw!'

'Something bad?' Kirstie guessed. 'So what was it?'

'A horse without a rider!' Hayley gave the details, her eyes round with shock. 'Troy stayed to try and capture the horse then find out what happened to the rider.'

'You did a great job!' Kirstie reassured the scared

106

sisters. 'So tell me, which horse did you see?'

Tessa drew a deep breath. 'It was Yukon!' she whispered. 'She was trailing her reins, kinda spooked and all wound up. But there was no Alicia. Kirstie, we think there's been a real bad accident out there in Aspen Park!'

8

Kirstie made the panicky Eastmann girls describe, as clearly as they could, the spot where they'd left Troy. Then she repeated Troy's instructions to them to let their horses show them the way home.

'Send people to help look for Alicia,' she told the girls. 'Ask if Ben can come, and maybe Hadley plus a couple more good riders.'

The sisters nodded and rode eagerly on.

Kirstie rode hard towards Aspen Park. She jumped felled trees, took short cuts across creeks – persuading Lucky to overcome his mistrust of the swollen water and hidden hollows that could plunge him belly deep into the ice-cold current.

Soon the park was in sight: a stretch of open grassland bounded by forest on three sides, all fenced in with razor-wire in an attempt to keep livestock in and deer out. To the fourth side there was one gate along a half-mile stretch of old-style rail-fencing, near to which stood a derelict log cabin with its roof caved in and only its stone chimney stack standing tall. Beyond the cabin was an even more beaten-up barn and a few more smaller wooden outbuildings that were little more than crumbling heaps.

At first it seemed to Kirstie that there were no horses or cattle inside the wide expanse of rough parkland. The meadow sloping up from the old cabin showed no signs of being trodden on, and red eagles soaring calmly overhead suggested no movements to catch their eye below.

But something, a sixth sense maybe, made her rein Lucky to a halt on the approaching ridge and watch the scene spread out below. The palomino too grew super-alert, flicking his ears and making the most of his almost 360 degree vision.

The green landscape was empty, and yet not. Kirstie felt a presence, a creature behind a tree or a rock, watching them. Which direction should she take? Was the creature friend or foe?

It was Lucky who took the doubt out of the situation. Listening, looking down from the ridge for maybe thirty seconds, he then threw back his golden, burnished head and let out a loud whinny.

In an instant there was an answering call.

Down behind the cabin, hidden from view!

'Let's go!' Kirstie whispered to Lucky, sitting deep in the saddle as her horse plunged downhill. She felt her cap fly from her head in the wind, but didn't stop to collect it. 'I'll bet you a hundred dollars it's Yukon playing hide-and-seek down there, so forget the cap and to heck with opening the gate. What we're gonna do is jump clean over the sucker!'

Lucky understood the leg commands and her touch on the reins. He galloped at the fence head-on, rose high in the air, soared over the rail and landed smoothly on the soft grass. Kirstie flexed her legs and lifted out of the saddle then eased herself down, reining Lucky to the right and making a wide circle round the back of the old homestead.

'Whoa!' she cried softly. Sure enough, there was Yukon, standing in the shadows eating sweet grass. When she raised her head to acknowledge them, Kirstie realised that her mane was dripping-wet.

'Great!' Kirstie breathed. Trust Yukon to ignore a crisis and focus on her stomach by feeding and drinking! 'What did you do with your rider?' she asked almost crossly as she urged Lucky to approach more closely.

But Yukon had found good pasture and didn't aim to be moved on before she'd had her fill. As Kirstie drew near, so she sidled away, alerted by the coil of lead-rope in Kirstie's hand to the fact that her unexpected leisure time in Aspen Park was due to come to an end.

'OK, OK, no time for games!' Kirstie muttered, just before she saw a long coil of rope snake through the air from the direction of the crumbling house. As the lasso dropped neatly over Yukon's head, Troy stepped into view.

'For a moment there I thought you and Lucky showin' up had messed up my plan!' He grinned at her surprise.

Yukon pulled and strained half-heartedly at the rope, then seemed to accept the inevitable. She heaved a big sigh and allowed Troy to hand over the end of the rope to Kirstie.

'What happened?' She secured the rope around her saddle horn and watched Troy lead Silver Spur out from behind the cabin. At least they had the loose horse back safe. Now all they needed to do was to track down Alicia.

'We found her soaked through and wandering loose and without a saddle . . .' Troy began, vaulting into the saddle to ride alongside.

'Yeah, I know. I saw the Eastmann girls. I mean, how come you ended up here?'

'Give this horse a medal!' Troy grinned, leaning forward to pat Silver Spur's neck. 'Yukon was real spooked when we first saw her. No way was she gonna hang around and get caught. So she lit out down the side of a deep draw and pretty soon I lost her in some aspens.

'But my horse here listened real good and he soon heard the mare calling out for a little company. They sure do hate being out alone in the big, cruel world.'

'So you followed the calls until you met up with Yukon here. Then what?' Even as she asked the question, Kirstie felt Yukon set up some resistance to being dallied on the end of a rope. The sturdy brown-and-white paint mare began to tug, not harshly but insistently towards the old barnlike structure behind the house.

'Then she went crazy again, kickin' out when I went to grab her reins.' From his position in the saddle, Troy's gaze began to rake the surrounding slopes, hoping for a sign of the missing rider. 'I had to back off and get ready to rope her in. That's when you and Lucky showed up.'

'OK, gotcha,' she confirmed, letting a little more slack into the dally rope as Yukon continued to pull and strain. 'And I rode out to tell you that the sheriff arrived early. So what do we do? Head back to the ranch or stay out to look for Alicia?'

'Stay out, no question.' Troy's reply came fast and firm. 'Listen, the kid could be lyin' out there injured. Maybe she broke a leg or a rib or somethin'. We can't up and leave her just so I can have my little chat with the sheriff.'

Quickly Kirstie agreed. 'OK, so we stay and figure this out. Listen, I know for a fact that Alicia set out late, just a few minutes before I did. So she must've pushed Yukon pretty hard across tough territory to get this far.'

'And she's not that great a rider,' Troy reminded her with a worried frown. They both noted out of the corner of their eyes that Yukon still refused to settle on the end of the dally. 'So suppose Alicia pushed her horse too far. Say Yukon refused to jump a log across the trail. That would be enough to cause the cinch to snap and the saddle to slide off. The next thing we know, the two Eastmann kids are spotting a loose horse and we have one injured rider lyin', maybe unconscious, God knows where!'

'Yeah, so there's only one player in this game that knows for sure where the accident happened, and that's Yukon,' Kirstie said quietly, beginning at last to pay proper attention to the brown-and-white paint. She saw now that the mare wasn't in fact pulling directly towards the broken-down barn, but to an animal track beaten in the long grass to one side, a path made by deer perhaps. In any case, Kirstie made up her mind to dismount and let Yukon lead her where she wanted to go.

'You reckon the horse can lead us to the girl?' Troy asked, dismounting likewise. 'Yeah, I guess maybe she even had it figured out to find me up on the ridge and lead me back down here!'

'Quit talking, will you?' Kirstie hissed, convinced by now that Yukon had led them with a clear purpose. A track made by wild deer usually led to a water source of some kind, and of course the log cabin would've been built on a site with running water nearby. 'There must be a creek over this next low ridge,' she told Troy, 'or a small lake maybe.'

Troy ran ahead of Kirstie and Yukon, cutting up to the top of the slope. 'Lake,' he reported, pointing out the curving track across the long grass which the deer had worn into the landscape.

And there, a quarter of a mile away, overlooked by quivering aspen trees Kirstie saw the shimmering stretch of water, a hundred yards long and twenty wide, fed by a clear running creek; all the water a homesteader could ever have wanted.

So Kirstie coiled up the dally rope and asked Troy for a leg up so she could ride Yukon bareback to the lake. Then the mare carried her at a steady lope, leaving the cowboy to follow on foot.

'You take us to Alicia!' Kirstie whispered in Yukon's ear, leaning forward and holding tight to the horse's mane. 'Clever girl to bring us to her. Yeah, good job!'

She pictured the novice rider pushing her horse too hard, enjoying the edge of danger involved in riding out alone into the great mountain range. And she recalled Alicia's sullen attitude, and the challenge that she herself had thrown as the visitor set off. 'Are you gonna tell the sheriff where you were when that locket got stolen, or am I?'

So Alicia would have been riding recklessly, curving round the edge of this hidden lake, making up time so she could join a group, scared maybe of what Sheriff Francini might uncover with his persistent, clear questioning. And she'd pushed it one step too far, leaned out of the saddle an inch too wide. She'd come to this sharp bend between a rock and a stand of aspens close to the water's edge, and somehow both horse and rider had ended up in the lake!

Yukon slowed to a trot and then a walk as they approached the dangerous bend. Then she stopped and turned her head towards the water.

'Jeez, Troy, it's Alicia!' Kirstie yelled. Panic seized her throat and almost choked her. There was a clear view of a body in the water, face-up, caught on the spike of a half-sunken tree trunk maybe a hundred yards from the shore. 'Get over here as fast as you can!'

And the level-headed cowboy, used to sudden emergencies out on the Montana ranges, gave a long, clean whistle to bring Silver Spur running from the shade of the derelict cabin.

Within seconds, Kirstie heard the thunder of hooves, sensed Troy leap into the saddle and found horse and rider at her side.

'Look!' she gasped, pointing to the lifeless body in the lake.

Troy nodded and pushed Silver Spur on into the water. The horse stumbled, found his footing, then waded deeper. 'Follow me!' he yelled over his

shoulder at Kirstie. 'I'm gonna need you!'

So she too urged Yukon forward, sliding from side to side of the mare's broad back as she waded unsteadily after Silver Spur. Soon the water reached the horses' bellies and soaked through the riders' boots and jeans. Then, moments later, the horses were out of their depth and swimming strongly towards the half-submerged trunk.

'Hold on!' Troy called, knowing that Kirstie was without reins or saddle horn to grip on to.

She linked her arms around Yukon's neck, laying her cheek against her mane, feeling the swift surge of the mare's body through the water. 'Did you see Alicia move?' she cried, hoping against hope that the girl had raised her arm to attract their attention.

'Yeah, but that could be just the action of the water swirling around her,' Troy reported from a little way ahead. 'The kid's probably unconscious. Maybe worse!'

So they ploughed on, the horses holding their nostrils clear of the smooth surface, long necks stretched forward, strong legs moving in a slow-motion lope through the deep, clear water.

At last, after two or three minutes, Troy and Kirstie reached the trunk that supported Alicia in a fork between two dead branches. They could see that her arm had hooked over one branch and that her body had wedged up against the main trunk, keeping her head above water. But her face was deadly white, her eyes closed and her mouth hanging half open.

It was Troy who reached her first. Leaning wide out of the saddle and grabbing a second broken branch with both hands, he swung himself from Silver Spur's back and up on to the slanted trunk. Then he inched along the rough, black bark towards the girl, crouching over her, head to one side to listen for breath.

'Yeah, she's alive!' he yelled to Kirstie who waited at a distance on Yukon while Silver Spur swam back towards them. Then Troy struggled into a position astride the tree trunk which allowed him to raise Alicia from her wedged position and cradle her against his chest. He felt her wrist for a pulse, nodded, then wrapped his arms around her middle, giving a tight, sudden squeeze which made her choke and gasp. Soon her eyes were opening and she was drawing in long, uneven gulps of air.

'Thank God!' Kirstie murmured. She felt her own held breath even out and she took hold of Silver Spur's trailing reins to edge him closer to the trunk once more.

'I'm gonna hand you over to Kirstie, OK?' Troy told Alicia in a loud, clear voice.

'Where am I? What happened?' she mumbled, struggling weakly to get out of Troy's grasp.

'You came off your horse. Somehow you landed out here, unconscious. Yukon came to fetch us.' Still Troy explained as if to a small child so that Alicia could get a hold on her surroundings. 'Now, what I plan to do is to get Kirstie to help you into Silver Spur's saddle and she can lead you back to the shore.'

'No!' Once more Alicia tried to resist.

But Troy simply lifted her from the trunk and held her in both arms out over the water so that Silver Spur could edge right up alongside. Then he eased her on to the horse's back, checked with Kirstie that she'd kept hold of the reins, then nodded at her to go ahead. 'I'll swim after you. See you on the shore!'

'Easy!' Kirstie told Yukon. The mare was starting to tire and toss her head around in the water. Spray from her mane whipped across Kirstie's hands and face as she turned to check that a woozy, confused Alicia was still secure on Silver Spur.

'I'm OK!' Alicia gasped, slumped forward but holding tight. 'Jeez, I'm sorry!' she whispered in a choked, small voice.

'Save that for later,' Kirstie told her, aware that Troy had dived into the water head first and was swimming up behind them. There would be plenty of time for explanations and apologies when they got back on to dry land.

'No, I really am sorry!' Soaked to the skin, hair plastered to her scalp, Alicia made a pitiful sight. 'I took it into my head I could make my horse swim in the lake. She didn't want to, but I made her. I was fooling around. Jeez, the horse has a better brain than I do!'

This time Kirstie said nothing.

'Did the sheriff leave the ranch yet?' Alicia asked, suddenly changing the subject.

They were ten yards from the bank. The horses were beginning to plant their hooves on the stony bed of the lake and wade unsteadily out of the water, nostrils flared, lungs gulping in huge gasps of air as their tired flanks heaved. 'Nope,' Kirstie said shortly. 'I came to get Troy. Sheriff Francini still wants to talk with him.'

Ironic, or what? she thought. The very guy they were all yelling 'Thief!' at was the one who just saved Alicia Rankin's bacon!

'Hmm,' Alicia sighed then grunted. Nothing else; just typical, silent, disgruntled Alicia.

* * *

'Arrest the guy!' John Pitts demanded in the full heat of the noonday sun.

Kirstie and Troy had delivered Alicia safely back to the arms of her mom. A doctor was on his way from town to check her over for the after-effects of concussion. Meanwhile, mother and daughter had retreated to Hummingbird to leave John to deal with the sheriff.

'You heard what he just said.' Francini stood up against the angry man. 'Hendren claims he's innocent.'

'Well he would, wouldn't he?' Growing more exasperated, Pitts breathed hot air and swung his arms around. 'No one's gonna admit to these thefts without the law putting some pressure on them first!'

Kirstie stood in the yard shoulder to shoulder with the accused cowboy, prepared to stake her life on his innocence. 'Where's the proof?' she demanded. 'C'mon, give me one shred of evidence. And don't tell me the Red Owen sob story about the missing rifle. That was all a big set-up, believe me!'

Hadley stood on the edge of the group, eyes narrowed, listening to Kirstie's outburst. He added

122

things up, tooks things away, said nothing.

John Pitts practically had steam coming out of his ears. 'Hendren had the perfect opportunity to steal Linda's locket!' he insisted, noting out of the corner of his eye that the Rankins were about rejoin them. 'He was there at the cabin at the time the theft took place!'

As Pitts turned to Linda for support, the mother allowed her daughter to step ahead of her into the middle of the group. It was Alicia who broke the silence at last.

'So was I,' she said quietly. 'I was there too.'

Yes! Kirstie's whole body relaxed in an instant. *And not before time!*

'Are you sure you're well enough to stand out here in the sun?' Larry Francini asked kindly, putting out a stout arm to support her slightly swaying figure.

Alicia pushed him away. 'Yeah, I'm sure. I spoke to Mom and she said I should get it all out in the open . . .' Faltering, Alicia slipped one hand into the pocket of her clean jeans and came out with an object that swung and glittered in the light.

'The stolen locket,' Francini murmured in a tone that conveyed the feeling of having seen it all in his time.

'Troy didn't steal it. Nobody did,' Alicia said, struggling to keep her voice going. The truth came out in broken chunks. 'Mom just left it lying by the coffee machine in the cabin . . . Well, she never does stuff like that . . . and I was angry when I saw it just lying around for anyone to steal. And it had my dad's picture in the middle of it, the last one he ever had taken . . . So anyway, I took it and hid it to teach her a lesson when she came back . . . Only then the whole thing got completely out of hand because Mom set up this big scene that the locket was stolen . . . and it was too late for me to own up . . . so I let it ride . . .'

'You let Troy get accused,' Kirstie whispered.

Taking a deep breath, Alicia nodded. 'I didn't like the guy. He wasn't nice to me when he fitted my saddle. But he just saved my life, and now I'm so ashamed I could die!'

It was Troy who stepped into the long, incredulous silence. 'It's OK, forget it,' he told Alicia. 'Everyone messes up once in a while.'

'That's mighty big of you,' the sheriff told him, turning to face Troy's second accuser. 'I guess that's one charge out of the way. Now sir, how about you?'

'I stand by what I said!' John Pitts insisted, his face full of thunder, his gaze aimed directly at Troy.

'No way did I steal my own camera, watch and seven hundred dollars in cash!'

9

'When did Ray Pickett leave?' Kirstie asked Sheriff Francini. Calves in need of branding were currently being brought in by Ben and Sandy, yet there was a space in the yard where the shoer's pick-up had been parked.

John Pitts had stormed off to his cabin, still convinced that Troy had picked up on the stolen-locket scare and used the opportunity to sneak in and raid the contents of his bedside cabinet. 'OK, so Hendren didn't take the darned pendant!' he'd admitted. 'And he just acted the hero out there on the lake. But you've still got the guy's shady past to deal with, and the fact that he has an open door to walk through any time there's no one looking!'

Larry Francini stood and watched Pitts's retreating figure, frowning slightly at Kirstie's odd question. 'What does Pickett have to do with any of this?'

'An IOU for $700!' Earnestly Kirstie delivered the key fact that she was convinced would clear up the whole mess. 'I saw a slip of paper in Ray's cab – he repaid a gambling debt for exactly that amount just yesterday!'

Francini nodded slowly, while Troy shot Kirstie a look to double-check that this wasn't a wind-up.

'This is no joke!' she insisted, and told them when and how it had happened. 'My hunch is that, given a little more time, I'd also have found a camera and a watch stashed away in Ray's glove-box!'

'Hold it,' Francini objected. 'The law doesn't operate on guesswork. We need solid facts.'

'But at least you should question Ray about the $700! That can't be coincidence, surely!'

Another slow nod from the sheriff indicated that, yes, he would sure like follow it up. So he leaned into his car and picked up the radio to make contact with his deputy. 'Hey, Ty; Larry here. I'd like you to put out a call to bring in a guy by the name of Ray

Pickett. Yeah, you got it, Ray Pickett. He runs a one-man, horse-shoeing outfit out of Marlowe County. Last seen driving a red and silver Dodge, heading out along the Half-Moon dirt road on to Route 3.'

'Forty-five minutes back,' Hadley put in quietly. 'I checked my wristwatch when I saw him drive out. Looked to me like he had an important appointment he couldn't afford to miss. I kinda wondered about it at the time.'

'Thanks, Hadley,' the sheriff acknowledged. 'Make that round twelve noon,' he told Ty. 'Hey, and check what we know about the guy's history, huh? Especially, look into any other big gambling debts he might've built up.'

'Horse-racing!' Kirstie cut in loudly. 'I spotted stacks of newspapers in his pick-up, all marked with runners he wanted to place money on.'

'You got that?' the sheriff asked his deputy. 'And look in on Focus, the camera shop on Marlowe County Main Street. I got a hunch that Pickett may have been dumb enough to trade in a used video camera recently. If so, we got some nice evidence there!'

'You see!' Kirstie turned gladly towards Troy. 'This is gonna work out fine!'

Even Hadley had the grace to step forward and

begin a mumbled apology for the part he'd played in incriminating Troy. 'I guess I jumped the gun back there,' he admitted. 'Shoulda kept it under my hat, thought about it, asked you straight out what took you up to Hummingbird Cabin that afternoon.'

'Forget it,' Troy told him. 'I've had Kirstie believin' in me from the start, like a guardian angel. Yeah, my golden-haired guardian angel!'

They were grinning together and Kirstie was blushing hard when the sheriff's voice interrupted them. 'Run that by me again, Ty. You say you just got an accident report five minutes back on a red Dodge – the pick-up spun off the road down a ravine? Could you give me an exact location on that, please!'

'Jeez!' Troy breathed, his face suddenly strained.

'Yeah, at the Eagle's Peak junction on Route 3, I got that.' Francini's manner too had snapped from laid back to urgent. 'The lady who reported the accident has given you a plate number. Check on the computer for the registered owner, OK ... Yeah, and the witness also says there's no sign of any driver in the pick-up. Got that too. Ty, I want you to get out to the scene pronto. I'll meet you there.'

By this time, Kirstie's head was spinning. One

minute, they were working towards a concrete case against the blacksmith, the next the guy was in a car wreck and had vanished!

'So, say Pickett got out of the smash.' Troy was thinking faster, consulting with the sheriff. 'Will you guys pick him up and hold him on suspicion?'

Francini had nothing to lose by admitting that this was his plan. 'First we gotta find him,' he said, quickly sliding his heavy bulk into his car. 'Any idea where he might be headed, Hadley?'

'In his shoes, I'd stick up my thumb and bum a lift into town,' the old wrangler replied bluntly. 'Then I'd rent me a hire car and head for the county line.'

'Could be. Stick around, will ya?' he told the three of them. 'Fill Sandy in when she gets back. A guy minus his mode of transport won't get far, so tell her we're close to making an arrest.'

With this, the sheriff cruised out of the yard for a thirty-minute drive to the scene of the accident.

'What if they don't pick Pickett up on Route 3?' Kirstie demanded anxiously. 'Maybe your idea's too obvious, Hadley. If he's smart, he'll head across country.'

'The guy ain't smart,' Hadley pointed out. 'Like Larry said, he's probably dumb enough to trade stolen goods, hoping he'll get away with it.'

'OK, so he's not the Brain of America, but he sure has to be desperate.' She had visions of the shoer picking himself up from the car wreck and staggering away from the scene on foot and with only one thing on his mind: he had to get away without being seen.

'You figure he got nervous and took off from here when he saw the sheriff?' Troy backtracked over events.

Kirstie nodded. 'I guess he got more and more twitchy. In the end, he must've panicked, figuring it wouldn't be long before the finger of suspicion was pointed his way.'

'Gotcha.' Troy lowered his head thoughtfully, then came up with a plan. 'What d'you say you and me ride out to the burn-out area west of Route 3?' he suggested to Kirstie. 'Can Silver Spur and Lucky bushwhack along Eagle's Peak Trail and reach the road before either the sheriff or his deputy make it by car?'

'Sure!' Kirstie didn't hesitate. Both horses were fast, sure-footed and rested after the lake incident. So she and Troy were already heading for the corral when Hadley called her back.

'Larry said to stick around here, remember!'

'You stay!' she yelled. 'Tell Mom what's going on. Troy and me will be more use joining in with the search!'

The old wrangler knew not to argue. He watched Troy and Kirstie jump into the saddle and head the horses out towards the creek, then called after them. 'If you find Pickett on the burn out and back him into a corner, no way will a guy like that put up his hands and come quietly. So you take care, OK!'

Hadley's warning followed them along Five Mile Creek Trail to Whiskey Rock. It hovered over their silent heads like a watchful hawk, sailing on currents of warm air, with them wherever they went.

'It'll be two against one,' Kirstie muttered, picturing the scene of confrontation: Pickett's sullen frown, the realisation that his game was finally up. All that she and Troy would need to do would be to keep him quietly at bay until the sheriff and his deputy turned up.

'Yeah, and he'll be shook up after the crash.' Troy sounded confident too, as he gave Silver Spur his head and set him into a lope across country.

Kirstie clicked her tongue for Lucky to follow, ducking low branches and picking a route between the ponderosa pines. Feeling the breeze on her face after the steady, dull heat of the valley, she felt herself waken up, ready for a confrontation with the runaway thief.

'Silver Spur's head is gonna be in a spin when we ask him to round up a guy instead of a steer,' Troy called back, checking the coil of rope slung over his saddle horn. 'Let's hope he can figure out what I want him to do!'

'He's a champion roping horse, ain't he?' she joked back, swerving to avoid the twisted stump of a tree that had been felled by lightning during a storm. Then swiftly she leaped over a shorn trunk which lay in their way. Lucky took the jump with ease, hooves thudding into the soft, sandy earth then pounding onwards.

'What happened with the burn-out?' Troy reined back his horse to wait for Kirstie. Ahead of him, stretching for a distance of two to three miles, lay an open landscape which rolled down dips and rose towards tall spikes of blackened tree stumps. Beyond that lay the fork in the main highway where Pickett's Dodge had dropped into the ravine.

'Forest fire over twenty years back,' she reported, scanning the empty scene. 'It was during my grandpa's time. Lost a lot of cattle. The whole patch was ablaze and it looked at one time like it might swallow up the ranch, only the wind changed direction and saved the house.'

The disaster had left behind a charred mountainside which had smouldered for weeks. Then the bare, scorched earth had gradually come back to life; young saplings had taken root the very next spring, aspens had grown between the ruined stumps and showed green amongst the black. Now, twenty years on, their shimmering green leaves and silver trunks softened the hillside, while willows crowded the valleys and creeks, providing cover for the wildlife that had returned.

'So, are you ready for one last lope?' Troy asked, checking his bearings by the height and direction of the sun.

'You bet.' This time she decided to lead Troy and Silver Spur along the most direct course to the fork in the road, choosing to swoop down the next hill, along an open stretch of grassland, and up to the next ridge, beyond which they would catch their first glimpse of the highway.

They came to another halt at the end of the ridge, gazing down to pick out the point at which Pickett had come off the road.

'There!' Troy murmured, pointing to a glint of metal, which on closer inspection turned out to be a reflection of sunlight from the upturned fender of the red Dodge. The vehicle must have careered off the carriageway on a sudden, sharp bend leading into the turn-off. It had plunged down a bank and turned on to its roof, crunching to a halt at the bottom of a shallow ravine.

'Pickett was lucky to get out of that alive!' Kirstie breathed. She noted that there were no other cars in sight, which meant that the sheriff and deputy hadn't yet made it to the scene. 'Should we check, just to make sure?'

Troy frowned then nodded. 'Maybe the witness made a mistake,' he agreed.

So they went ahead, trotting more cautiously now, stopping occasionally to look for signs in the dirt that Ray Pickett had in fact got out and walked away. But neither Kirstie nor Troy spied a single bootprint in the scrubland around the ravine.

'I don't like this!' Taking a deep breath, Troy admitted to feeling uneasy as they drew close to the wreck. 'What if the guy is trapped under there, out of sight?'

'Don't!' Kirstie shuddered. Now she stopped looking for footprints and started searching for pools of blood seeping out from under the crushed truck.

Here in the bottom of the draw, the sun seemed hotter and the cooling breeze ceased. The two horses seemed reluctant to go on, tossing their heads and sidestepping as their riders urged them forward.

They were ten yards from the wreck, studying the track gouged into the earth by the truck as it had left the highway and plunged into the draw. First there were tyre marks, then a section of churned earth and uprooted bushes, then a stretch of scraped rock leading to a ledge where the pick-up must have tipped on to its side and begun to roll. A smashed mirror lay on the rock; shards of glass and pieces of crumpled metal littered the lower slope.

'Hold it right there!' a voice ordered.

Troy and Kirstie twisted around to squint into the dazzling sun.

The silhouette of a man standing feet wide apart on a high rock spooked their horses and made them start sideways.

'I said, hold it!' Pickett repeated.

And this time, the long barrel of a hunting rifle raised to his shoulder, pointing straight at them, came sharply into focus.

Kirstie and Troy froze. Lucky and Silver Spur tensed up and flattened their ears. *Danger. Predator nearby. Get ready to run.*

'I guess Little Miss Poke-Her-Nose-In didn't tell you I carried a gun in my truck!' Pickett sneered, without moving down from his perch. 'Hunting's my favourite leisure activity, next to losing dough at the race track!'

'You leave Kirstie out of this!' Troy replied. 'This is between you and me.'

'Yeah, but she's your number one fan. Sooner or later she was gonna nail me for the Pitts thing, the amount of snoopin' around she's been doin'.'

'I already did!' Kirstie called back defiantly. 'Sheriff Francini's on his way right now!'

'See!' Pickett gave a hollow laugh. Keeping the gun aimed squarely on Troy, he began to sidle off the rock and make his way down to their level.

As he drew nearer and came out of the direct line of the sun, Kirstie could see that the flesh on the smith's right forearm was gashed and scraped from the accident. And he limped on his right ankle, dragging his foot in the dirt.

'That's how come he never moved away from the scene!' she whispered to Troy, wincing at the sight of blood trickling down Pickett's hand on to the butt of his gun.

'Cool it!' Troy warned the advancing man. 'This gun stuff ain't gonna get you nowhere!'

Pickett was ten yards away, still aiming, and with a reckless grin on his dirt-covered face. 'It sure is!' he sneered, tapping the steel barrel. 'This here gun is gonna get me clean out of here!'

'No way!' Troy argued steadily, easing across Kirstie and Lucky's path so that he stood full square in front of them. Silver Spur's ears were back, his whole instinct was still to flee. Even so, he did as Troy asked.

Pickett stopped and swayed, letting the sweat pour unchecked from his forehead, down his smeared cheeks. 'Sure it is,' he insisted. 'Listen mister, you're gonna step right down from that saddle and hand over your horse. I know that four legs ain't nowhere near as good as four wheels, which is what I've been waitin' for along this God-forsaken stretch of road. But right now it's the best I can do!'

'Dream on, buddy!' Troy retorted. He didn't move a muscle to dismount. 'This horse knows to take orders from only one rider, and that's me!'

'I said, get down!' Pickett jerked the rifle and hooked his forefinger round the trigger.

'Troy, do as he says!' Kirstie was convinced that Pickett must be out of his skull with pain and fear. The guy had a wild look in his eyes; he was definitely out of control.

Ignoring her, Troy clicked his tongue and dug his heels gently into Silver Spur's sides.

The paint edged forward – one step, two, three . . .

'I mean it!' Pickett cried, adjusting his aim as Troy advanced. 'I'll shoot if you make another move!'

'Yeah, I'm real scared!' Troy laughed in his face. 'A punk like you is gonna blast me out of the saddle, is he? Go ahead, do it!'

'Man, I will, I'll do it!' the smith screamed in a high-pitched voice. But his hands had begun to shake, and when he squeezed the trigger, his aim was all wrong.

Kirstie heard the blast of a shotgun at close quarters. She saw Silver Spur rear up and squeal with pain.

Then there was blood.

A crimson fountain spurted from the horse's shoulder as he fell forward and sank to the ground. He was on his knees, gasping, raising his head and struggling to get back up as the blood ran freely to the sandy red earth.

Troy slid from the saddle as Silver Spur collapsed on to his side.

And a terrified Pickett was scrambling back up to his rocky perch, shoving a new cartridge into place and getting ready to aim the gun full square in Kirstie's face.

10

'Your turn!' the shoer yelled. 'Now you hand over
your palomino, or I shoot him as well!'

Kirstie heard the threat and saw the rifle. Out of
the corner of her eye she saw Troy crouch over Silver
Spur, take off his shirt and use it to stem the flow
of blood from the gunshot wound. The horse lay
quiet on his side, breathing heavily.

'What d'you gain by shooting my horse?' she
yelled back, stalling for time. 'That leaves you with
no chance of a getaway.'

'You think I won't do it?' Pickett threatened. Back
up on the rock, his back to the sun, the gunman's

141

face was in deep shadow. Having reached a safe ledge, he laughed cynically as a new thought struck him. 'Hey, I'm a gambling man, remember. What money would you put on Lucky coming through this alive?'

'Nothing. I'm not betting anything.' Kirstie kept the panic out of her voice, deciding not to try Troy's method of challenging Pickett head-on. Instead, she planned to play for still more time.

'Listen, I figure you could shoot him dead without a second thought, just like Silver Spur. And no way am I gonna risk it.'

Let him think the paint had been fatally wounded. In fact, Troy's first-aid seemed to be working. The blood had stopped flowing from what turned out to be a shallow flesh wound.

'Yeah, you love your palomino!' Pickett sneered. 'I figured I could count on that!'

'Right, so come on, take him!' she offered. 'Just promise me you won't harm him after you've made your getaway. Leave him somewhere safe, so I can come along and pick him up later.'

The shoer heard the deal, but kept the gun aimed dead at Kirstie. 'How do I know you mean it?' he asked suspiciously.

'You have to believe me,' she urged, slipping from

the saddle and standing alongside Lucky. Then she held up the reins towards him. 'C'mon; isn't this what you want?'

'No tricks?'

'I'm giving it to you straight. Take my horse!'

Come down to ground level. Stop pointing that gun in my face, Kirstie silently pleaded.

'Keep him talking!' Troy hissed, crouching out of Pickett's line of vision, satisfied now that Silver Spur was out of danger. Carefully he worked his way under an overhang on the rock which the shoer was using as his lookout perch and reached out to release the coiled rope from the paint's saddle horn.

'If you cheat me, you're dead!' Pickett warned, letting the gun drop slightly. He made his first move to descend the twenty feet from the top of the rock.

'You gotta make it fast!' Kirstie insisted. 'The sheriff could arrive any second!'

Make him even more stressed out, make him stumble on the injured ankle. Make him fall.

But no; Pickett found his painful way down to the ground. He didn't see Troy crouched under the overhang, only Silver Spur lying in the dirt, not moving.

'OK, gimme the reins!' The smith snatched at them, throwing himself off balance. But he

staggered and righted himself, pushing Kirstie to one side with the long gun barrel so that she fell against a thorn bush.

Troy waited in the shadows, watching Pickett struggle into the saddle with one good leg. He grunted and groaned as his injured ankle and arm took some of the strain.

C'mon, Troy; jump the guy now, before he gets away!

Kirstie pulled herself free of the spiky bush. 'Leave Lucky in a place where I can find him,' she pleaded, as if she really was prepared to let him ride away.

'Don't hold your breath!' Pickett sneered, his rifle resting across the front of the saddle.

With a casual glance at Silver Spur lying in the dust, he pulled roughly at Lucky's reins.

The palomino jerked his head and wheeled to the side.

'Hey, Troy, you can quit playin' hide-and-seek!' Pickett had caught sight of the wrangler hiding under the rock. He couldn't resist taunting him one last time.

Too late! I tried to set it up so you could jump him, but you waited too long! Kirstie's hopes dived lower than ever.

'Come on outta there, mister! Since when did a

macho guy like you hide from the action?' One hand resting on the gun-butt, Pickett crowed at Troy. 'Come and watch me ride into the sunset, like in the old movies!'

Slowly Troy emerged, hands behind his back, white T-shirt streaked with dust and blood. His eyes never moved from Pickett's hand on the gun.

Pickett grinned. 'Adios! Ain't that what they say? Adios, amigos!'

As he reined Lucky harshly for a second time, ready to ride off into the burn-out, Kirstie's horse leaned back on his strong haunches and raised his front hooves off the ground. The action made Pickett slide back in the saddle and grab for the horn, simultaneously letting the rifle tilt. But he caught hold of it before it slipped away and he used the wooden butt to twist around and whack Lucky across the back.

'Now!' Kirstie yelled at Troy.

Lucky staggered under the heavy blow, throwing his rider further off balance. The horse kicked and bucked, raising dust and lashing out in pain.

Troy brought his lasso from behind his back. He raised the loop, aimed it at Pickett and threw.

Kirstie watched the rope arc through the air and fall short of the shoer's head and shoulders. For a split second she thought the unthinkable: Troy had missed!

But no. The cowboy had been aiming for the gun which Pickett still brandished in his left arm. It snaked over the barrel as Lucky kicked and bucked. Troy pulled. The noose tightened around the gun. He pulled again and jerked the weapon clean out of Pickett's hand.

'Which leaves me minus a blacksmith!' Sandy Scott told Glen Woodford, finding time at last to give the vet a full account.

It was two days later and Kirstie was present when Glen called at the ranch to check the sutures in Silver Spur's flesh wound. Sandy had told him the whole story: how she and Ben had arrived on the scene in time to mop up the mess, long after the real action had finished.

'I find my daughter with a hunting rifle in her hands, pointing it at the guy I just employed to shoe my horses!' she explained. 'And my wrangler is socking my shoer in the jaw, knocking him senseless, just as the sheriff drives up from the other direction to arrest him.'

'Arrest who? The wrangler?' Glen heard it all without pausing in his work. He gave Silver Spur a shot of antibiotics and checked that the wound was healing well.

'No, the shoer. It's like something out of a Jesse James story: outlaws, showdowns!' Sandy stood by, arms folded, acting like she was mad at Kirstie, but really grinning at her and having a joke. 'Not only that, but the horse has taken a bullet in the shoulder and the place is covered in blood!'

'And did Pickett admit the theft when they took him in?' Glen asked, straightening up after he'd packed his bag. The regular visitor to Half-Moon Ranch gave the impression that nothing surprised him.

'Yep. Which gives me one satisfied dude by the name of John Pitts,' Sandy confirmed. 'The sheriff recovered his camera from the dealers in Marlowe County and his watch from a jewellers down the street. Pickett made a statement pointing out the pressure he was under to repay some big debts; he reckons he cracked under the strain, that he wouldn't normally steal.

'But Larry Francini checked his record in a couple of other states, and found he'd done two six-month gaol terms for similar offences!' Sandy raised her eyebrows and shrugged. 'Like I say, I'm minus one shoer!'

'And maybe minus one wrangler.' Glen nodded his head towards his Jeep parked in the yard, where Troy stood deep in conversation with a woman Kirstie had never seen before.

'Give me a break!' Sandy muttered, shaking her head and leading the vet to the barn to check a couple of cows with foot problems.

'So who's the woman?' Kirstie demanded before Glen had time to follow. 'Did she drive in with you?'

'Yep. That lady is Mary Lee Stewart. She fixed up a ride out here with me. And boy, is she the type who knows what she wants!'

Mary Lee Stewart? The name rang a bell for Kirstie, but she couldn't place it exactly. So she decided to wander over to the house and hang around in the porch, where maybe she would learn more.

'We ended the week with a full head count!' Troy was telling the visitor. 'Just this morning, we checked two hundred steers through the gate into the holding-pen. Yes ma'am, we rounded up every single one!'

'Good job,' Mary Lee murmured. She looked like one of those hard-headed women who spend their lives managing cattle and male ranch hands, riding the range to check that the outfit is running smoothly. Dressed in a man's checked shirt, with faded blue jeans and tan boots, her greying hair was cut short and her one ornament was an embossed silver buckle on her wide leather belt.

'I hear your first week wasn't easy,' she continued, shrewdly looking Troy up and down. 'When I was in town, they told me a girl nearly drowned in the lake, a guy snuck in and stole a whole load of stuff and your horse even got a bullet in him.'

'Yeah, the vet's with Silver Spur right now.'

Kirstie noticed that Troy deliberately avoided giving the visitor any details about the part he'd played. In fact, rather than boasting and being full of himself, he seemed ready to shrug the whole thing off.

'Will you make the contest in Dallas next month?' Mary Lee asked.

'Yes ma'am. I aim to be there.'

'But you'll miss out on training until Silver Spur gets fit again?'

'Yes, ma'am.'

'I have a great cutting horse you could use at the Double E . . .' she told him.

Kirstie watched Troy frown and heard him clear his throat. Now, at the mention of the ranch name, she placed Mary Lee Stewart as the owner of a big spread in Montana. Of course; she was the woman who had wanted to hire Troy earlier in the spring!

'And I'd be working cattle for you on the north range?' Troy double-checked on something the ranch boss had mentioned earlier. 'I'd have a couple of guys under me, and I'd be head-man?'

She nodded. 'You do your own thing. In your free time you get to train your cutting horse.'

Kirstie took a deep breath and sat down hard on the porch step. It sounded like Mary Lee Stewart had waltzed in with an offer Troy couldn't refuse. *So this is what Glen had meant by her mom being minus one wrangler!*

'And you don't pay attention to the bad stories about me?' Troy reminded her of Red Owen's campaign to blacken his name.

Mary Lee grinned. 'Do I look like a woman who forms an opinion on some other guy's hearsay?'

'No,' he acknowledged, noticing Kirstie for the first time and beginning to blush under his deep tan.

'Listen,' Mary Lee went on. 'I never believed any of that stuff. That's why I'm here in Colorado, tracking you down to ask you nicely if you'd be good enough to come and work for me at the Double E. Because good cutters and ropers are hard to find, and from what I saw of you in the contest in New Jersey, you, Troy Hendren, are one of the best!'

'Thank you, ma'am,' Troy muttered shyly.

('Yeah, Troy was *shy*!' Kirstie insisted later to Sandy and Matt. 'I know; difficult to believe, huh?')

'So, how about it?' Mary Lee pushed him to make a decision there and then. 'Don't make me wait until after Dallas; I want you to come and work for me now!'

'Which was how come I was at Denver International Airport late yesterday,' Kirstie told Lisa in school on the following Monday.

Troy had shaken hands with Mary Lee Stewart on the deal and the ranch boss had gone away satisfied.

'Jeez, that must be the world speed record for taking a job and leaving it again!' Lisa sympathised.

'I know, but what could we do?'

Troy had taken Kirstie to one side and tried to explain. 'Cowboying is my life,' he'd said. 'The real stuff, not the dude version. Getting tired and dirty out on the range, sleeping rough, cuttin' cattle, ropin' them in. The truth is, I'm better working with cows than people!'

Kirstie had smiled but not hidden her

disappointment. 'The way I look at it, you were great with both.'

'Your mom will get another wrangler,' Troy had insisted gently. 'I hear Brad has come up with a couple more names for her.'

'It won't be the same.'

'That's true. Nothing ever is. But that's life.'

So she'd had to accept that Troy was leaving, and had even offered to drive to the airport with her mom to see him off.

Weird, she thought, how well you got to know a guy within the space of one short week.

This was while he was shaking hands all round, smiling at her, then striding through the crowds towards his check-in gate, head and shoulders taller than the rest.

Another goodbye.

'But at least we get to keep Silver Spur for a couple of weeks,' Kirstie told Lisa on the Monday.

'How come?'

'He stays with us until his wound completely heals, then Matt and I get to trailer him out to Montana.'

'Cool,' Lisa said.

'Troy says I can ease him back into work this time next week, help get him into shape for Dallas.'

'Neat. Can I come and watch?'

'Sure.' Kirstie stood up at the sound of the lesson bell, her spirits rising as she pictured Silver Spur. 'I tell you, this horse may not be great appearance-wise. In fact, he looks kinda dopey.'

She recalled Troy's pride and joy standing sleepily at the meadow fence that very morning, heavy head nodding, eyelids drooping at the comings and goings on Half-Moon Ranch.

'But wait 'til you see him cut and rope,' she told Lisa. 'Man, his hooves don't hardly touch the ground!'

HORSES OF HALF-MOON RANCH
Moondance

Jenny Oldfield

New arrival Moondance is a sale barn
bargain; beautiful but only half schooled.
Hadley blames rival dude owner, Ty Tyler,
for the blue roan's bad habits and poor
condition. Kirstie shares the old wrangler's
doubts over Tyler's claims for his magical
horse-training method. But she's not happy
when Hadley rides into a head-on
confrontation which could put both his and
Moondance's lives at risk . . .

HORSES OF HALF-MOON RANCH
Jenny Oldfield

0 340 71616 9	1: WILD HORSES	£3.99	❏
0 340 71617 7	2: RODEO ROCKY	£3.99	❏
0 340 71618 5	3: CRAZY HORSE	£3.99	❏
0 340 71619 3	4: JOHNNY MOHAWK	£3.99	❏
0 340 71620 7	5: MIDNIGHT LADY	£3.99	❏
0 340 71621 5	6: THIRD-TIME LUCKY	£3.99	❏
0 340 75727 2	7: NAVAHO JOE	£3.99	❏
0 340 75728 0	8: HOLLYWOOD PRINCESS	£3.99	❏
0 340 75729 9	9: DANNY BOY	£3.99	❏
0 340 75730 2	10: LITTLE VIXEN	£3.99	❏
0 340 75731 0	11: GUNSMOKE	£3.99	❏
0 340 75732 9	12: GOLDEN DAWN	£3.99	❏
0 340 77868 7	JETHRO JUNIOR	£3.99	❏
0 340 77965 9	STARLIGHT	£3.99	❏

All Hodder Children's books are available at your local bookshop, or can be ordered direct from the publisher. Just tick the titles you would like and complete the details below. Prices and availability are subject to change without prior notice.

Please enclose a cheque or postal order made payable to *Bookpoint Ltd*, and send to: Hodder Children's Books, 39 Milton Park, Abingdon, OXON OX14 4TD, UK. Email Address: orders@bookpoint.co.uk

If you would prefer to pay by credit card, our call centre team would be delighted to take your order by telephone. Our direct line *01235 400414* (lines open 9.00 am–6.00 pm Monday to Saturday, 24 hour message answering service). Alternatively you can send a fax on *01235 400454*.

TITLE		FIRST NAME		SURNAME	

ADDRESS	

DAYTIME TEL:		POST CODE		

If you would prefer to pay by credit card, please complete: Please debit my Visa/Access/Diner's Card/American Express (delete as applicable) card no:

Signature .... Expiry Date: ....

If you would NOT like to receive further information on our products please tick the box. ❏